What the critics are saying...

Five stars "This story is beautifully written and I was utterly impressed by *Ms. Kingston's* creativity in creating this remarkable tale. Through the development of the relationship between the main characters, the author provides just enough foreshadowing to keep the reader engrossed. Princess Riva is a woman determined to do anything to save her father and her land, but she learns more about herself than she ever bargained for." ~ *Laci Grey, Just Erotic Romance Reviews*

Four Stars "In this moving story, which has sympathetic characters and steamy sex, *Kingston* has written an explicit book with bondage, multiple partners and spanking. The first in a series, this is a wonderful fantasy that has both action and emotion." ~ *Page Traynor, Romance Times*

"*Katherine Kingston* has written an engrossing, erotic tale with plenty of sexual encounters, fantasies, and discipline. Her deft depiction of Princess Riva's growth seems believable, and is satisfying...Her writing style is unobtrusive, and she stays in Princess Riva's point of view throughout...Since there were three objects of quests, and no one person could obtain more than one, I hope that *Ms. Kingston* will continue the saga with Princess Riva's brother and sister." ~ *Nancy Riggins-Hume, The Road to Romance*

Katherine Kingston

SilverQuest

ELLORA'S CAVE
ROMANTICA PUBLISHING

An Ellora's Cave Romantica Publication

www.ellorascave.com

Silverquest

ISBN # 1419950789
ALL RIGHTS RESERVED.
Silver Quest Copyright© 2004 Katherine Kingston
Edited by: Briana St. James
Cover art by: Syneca

Electronic book Publication: January, 2004
Trade paperback Publication: December, 2005

Excerpt from *Bronzequest* Copyright © Katherine Kingston, 2005
Excerpt from *Healing Passion*
Copyright © Katherine Kingston, 2004

Warning:

The following material contains graphic sexual content meant for mature readers. *Silver Quest* has been rated *E-rotic* by a minimum of three independent reviewers.

Ellora's Cave Publishing offers three levels of Romantica™ reading entertainment: S (S-ensuous), E (E-rotic), and X (X-treme).

S-*ensuous* love scenes are explicit and leave nothing to the imagination.

E-*rotic* love scenes are explicit, leave nothing to the imagination, and are high in volume per the overall word count. In addition, some E-rated titles might contain fantasy material that some readers find objectionable, such as bondage, submission, same sex encounters, forced seductions, etc. E-rated titles are the most graphic titles we carry; it is common, for instance, for an author to use words such as "fucking", "cock", "pussy", etc., within their work of literature.

X-*treme* titles differ from E-rated titles only in plot premise and storyline execution. Unlike E-rated titles, stories designated with the letter X tend to contain controversial subject matter not for the faint of heart.

Also by Katherine Kingston:

Silverquest
Glimmer Quest

Prologue

In another time and place, a king ruled a small but prosperous kingdom called Serendonia.

It was a delightful place, full of happy people who enjoyed a comfortable existence. They worked hard, but the land rewarded their labor with plentiful harvests. Animal stock provided eggs, milk, and meat in abundance. A wide diversity of vegetables and fruits thrived.

All was well in Serendonia, until the day King Warren had a nasty mishap while helping with the shearing of the sheep. Kings don't normally spend much time in such humble tasks, but King Warren liked to help out where he could, since his very small, placid kingdom didn't require much work to keep it running. And while he was shearing a ram, the blade slipped and sliced an ugly, deep wound in his thigh.

The local healer came to tend him. She cleaned the injury as best she could, sewed it up, and packed it with healing herbs, then she said a few prayers over it.

Despite her best efforts, the wound refused to heal. Though it did not become morbid, the injury would not close completely. The king bled constantly. He grew weak and was in constant pain. His family called in sorcerers who worked spell after spell, but nothing helped.

As though in sympathy, the land itself became ill also. The rain refused to fall. Streams dried up, plants withered, animals died, and harvests grew thinner.

The king worried and fretted. His own discomfort he could bear, but to see his people suffering from hunger and malaise pained him beyond bearing. Since he could no longer help with the more active tasks, he spent his time in the library, searching for an answer to his problem.

When they could, one or the other of his three adult, unmarried children helped him. But none of them were there the day he finally found the answer he sought.

It was no easy answer. He had to think long and hard about what he'd learned before he finally called his children together.

Chapter One

Stirring the pot of fruit preserves didn't require much of her attention, so Princess Riva found her mind wandering, as it so often had lately, to her favorite dreams and the man who came to her in them.

As usual, he wore a mask obscuring his features. Only his eyes, an unusual light brown color, almost gold, showed from the slits cut into the black fabric hiding his face.

Though the light was dim, she could discern the graceful outline of his body. Wide shoulders and strong chest narrowed to a slim waist. He moved with a supple precision that came from finely honed muscles.

From where she lay on the bed, she watched him approach. Fear warred with desire. She was a prisoner – his prisoner – but the emotion that made her stomach clench and her heartbeat race whenever he came close wasn't entirely fear. He reminded her of a tiger, large, beautiful, and dangerous.

"So, Princess," he said as he approached. "Have you thought about my proposal?" His voice sent shivers flying up and down her spine. It was rich, deep, smooth, and dark.

"There is naught to consider," she tossed back at him. "You've had my answer. It will not change."

"Nay?" He came closer, moving to the side of her bed. "I could claim by force what you refuse to give willingly."

Her breath caught in her throat. Something told her he wouldn't truly force her. But a sneaky, traitorous part of her almost wished he would.

Hoping to catch him unprepared, she jumped up off the bed, pushed him hard enough to make him stumble and fall on his rear, and ran for the door he'd left standing open. Her bare feet slid on the flagstone floors. She made it only a little way down the hall before a hand fell on her shoulder. She stumbled.

An arm circled her waist, supporting and trapping her. "Nay, Princess. I'll not force myself on you, yet neither will I allow this to go unanswered."

He lifted her easily into his arms and held her securely despite her struggles as he carried her back into the cell. He sat on the side of the bed, still cradling her in his arms. Against her will she leaned into his chest, thrilling to the solid muscles there and his male scent.

Her compliance didn't last long when he shifted his grip and flipped her over, landing her across his knees. She yelled and wriggled when his hand slapped down on her bottom. It burned where he smacked her. He ignored her struggles to get off his lap, just tightening an arm around her to hold her in place as he whacked her rear end steadily. Nor did he pay attention to her moans, cries, squeals, screams, or pleas for mercy.

It hurt, but beneath the pain, a tingling excitement spread out through her body, born in her stinging derriere.

He spanked her for a long time, until her bottom felt like a blazing inferno raged there, and her tears flowed freely. She wanted it to stop, but she thrilled to his strength and mastery. He halted abruptly and rolled her over, then pulled her back into his arms, holding her against his chest while she cried.

She should be fighting him, but she couldn't bring herself to do so. Though her derriere burned fiercely, another ache wound its way into her, an ache of need pressing in her loins. Her body burned with desire for him.

When she calmed a bit, he gently tipped her head back and looked at her. With his fingers, he brushed away the tears. Then he lowered his face and his lips skimmed tenderly along her temple, her cheek, across her mouth to her jaw, and down along her throat, leaving streaks of tingling skin wherever his mouth touched.

He drew back a moment, then slanted his mouth over hers and lingered there for a long, drugging kiss. Heat roused inside and poured along her veins. His tongue brushed against her lips and nudged them apart. Fire ignited in her and she strained toward him, seeking to deepen the kiss and press her body tighter to his.

His hands moved from their resting spot on her shoulders, brushing down along her arms and then across to her breasts…

"Your Highness!"

Riva was jerked abruptly out of the glorious daydream at the sound of the voice demanding her attention. It took a moment to reorient herself. Secretly mourning the interruption of the thrilling fantasy, she turned to the woman frowning at her. "Aye, Mariana. What is it?"

"Your Highness," the woman repeated. "His Majesty, your father, summons you to his presence."

A shaft of fear shot through her. "Is His Majesty unwell?"

"Nay, Your Highness. No worse than ever."

Riva sighed in relief. "Take charge of stirring the fruit for me, if you will, Mariana. I believe it's close to done." She handed off the spoon and hurried out, stripping off her apron as she went.

She sighed away the remnants of her fantasy, for fantasy it was, in truth. None of the men presented to her as eligible candidates for her hand appealed to her in the least. Though some were good-looking, and one of those even rather amiable, none had the forcefulness and confidence she sought, nor the ability to master her which she hungered for. Though she did not try to be overbearing or show openly her strength of will, she nonetheless knew she intimidated most men.

As she neared her father's private chamber, she met her younger brother and sister, coming from the other direction. Both looked worried.

"You were summoned as well?" Riva asked.

"Aye," John answered.

"Is he worse?" Worry pulled Lia's pretty face into a frown.

"I was told no. I shouldn't think he would deteriorate so quickly in any case. Just this morning when I talked with him, he seemed no worse than before."

"I wonder why he would summon all three of us at once, then," John said.

"We'll soon learn." Upon arriving at the chamber door, Riva knocked and was admitted by a man-at-arms.

The three of them bowed to the man who held himself straight and proud in the chair near the bed. John had worked closely with the carpenter to build the chair for maximum comfort and recruited several seamstresses to add pillows to soften its seat and back.

"Riva, John, Lia," he said, smiling at each in turn. "My thanks for being so prompt. Do come here and sit down, my dears."

A series of chairs lined a wall of the room. Since the King's injury, he often conducted the business of state in this chamber.

"Are you well, Father?" Riva asked. She and Lia both approached him and kissed his forehead before taking their seats.

"No better than I've been for the last months," he admitted. "But no worse, either." He paused and looked down at a book on the desk nearby. "I think I may have found an answer for this, however."

"An answer?" Lia asked. "Something that might cure you, sir?"

"Aye," he said. His fond smile faded quickly. "I fear it means I must ask each of you to do a great favor for me."

"You know you have but to ask, Father," Riva said.

A corner of his mouth crooked up again. "Be not so quick to say so, my dear. It would be no small thing demanded of each of you should you choose to undertake this venture."

"Do tell us what is needed," Riva begged.

"I've been reading the legends from our world and many other parallel worlds." The King paused and sighed. "There's little else I can do, trapped here by this." He patted the mound of bandages on his thigh, then turned brisk again, dismissing his moment of despair.

"I've found a legend I think may provide an answer. It's from a parallel world, but one that overlaps ours in many areas. Three powerful objects are hidden within our worlds, but in times of need, strong people can claim them for healing purposes."

His gaze moved over all three of them. "My reading leads me to believe that if we can retrieve all three objects and bring them here, they may be able to heal this, and repair the damage to our lands as well."

Riva glanced at her brother and sister. She read in their faces the same resolve she felt. "We will retrieve those objects for you, Father."

He gave them a sad smile. "Nay, be not so quick to promise, my love. Though I do thank you for it. There is more to the legend than I've yet told you. 'Tis not so easy to find or claim these objects. The tales speak of difficult journeys, with many obstacles and trials along the way. And even when the seeker finds his goal, there are tests within tests yet to be passed. Many who seek these objects fail, and often failure brings death. I would have you think very carefully before you offer to do this. In truth, I would be happier if you could suggest others you would trust to do this for us." He stopped to draw a long breath. "My reading of the tales indicates those who have the most reason to want or need the objects for purely unselfish reasons are most likely to succeed. The person to claim these things must be pure of heart, courageous, loving, loyal, and honorable."

His expression turned sad and strained. "I have debated long whether to tell you of this possibility. It burns my heart to think of anyone undertaking these quests. The danger is great. The objects—three of them—are in different locations, guarded by strong wards, and each must be retrieved by a different individual, so no one person may undertake all three quests. I truly hope each of you can find someone worthy for this task, though I know in truth you three are closer to the ideals than any others I know."

Riva looked at John and Lia again. The determination on their faces mirrored what she felt. "We can and will do this thing, Father," she said, speaking for all of them. "We are your daughters and son. Who else has the power we've got from you, or the strength of love?"

Lines of doubt and unhappiness deepened in his face. "I know not, but I would prefer you found others, people you trust, to do this."

Riva considered candidates she knew who might be able to complete such a quest. A few of their knights came to mind, yet all had flaws that would seem to rule them out. Sir Aldwyn had great heart, but he was too old and getting weak. Sir Farriel was strong but an unrepentant womanizer. Sir Trayford had lately become too fond of strong drink. And withal, none would feel as great a need and desire for the objects as did she and her brother and sister.

"We'll try to find people we trust to do this," she said.

Chapter Two

Her horse slowed on an uneven spot of road. Riva wiped a bead of sweat off her forehead and reached for the waterskin. After three weeks of travel, she was weary and sore, and praying it wasn't much farther to her destination. She hadn't seen a town since she'd left the inn at the last one the previous morning. A night spent on the ground hadn't improved her humor.

While she grumbled to herself, they crested a hill. She brought her mount to a halt and surveyed the landscape. The road dove down and twisted around the side of a rise before it emerged from trees and hills off to her left onto a flatter plain. She followed its direction with her eye. A distant gleam of water flashed. Looking up a bit, she glimpsed the tip of a spire.

Riva breathed a sigh of relief and nudged the horse forward and down the hill. By late afternoon, she'd reached the banks of the river separating her island destination from the mainland. There she encountered her first test. The road appeared to end right at the side of the stream with no way across the water. A quick scan in either direction showed no bridge in sight.

She dismounted. A short search turned up a broken branch near the water. When she pushed it in to test the depth, it didn't appear to hit the bottom. She sighed, walked back to the road, and got back on the horse.

Long excursions north and south of the road, following the path of the water, revealed no means of crossing. She returned to the road and sat down on a rock nearby to consider the problem.

The spires of the castle loomed tantalizingly over the trees on the other side of the river. The slanting rays of the late afternoon sun reflected off the tops of the towers in gleams of gold and copper.

She was missing something. The road went straight to the water's edge. Why would it do that if there were no way across? She got up and walked to the side of the river, then paced off a little ways downstream.

It still took a moment or two before she noticed that the air over the water seemed to shimmer in a peculiar way in one spot. When she saw the odd waver, though, she picked up the stick she'd used earlier, walked to the edge of the river where the shimmer would intersect with land, and pushed.

The stick hit a flat, though invisible, surface, and tapped against it. Now that she knew it existed and where it was, Riva whispered a few words of a simple incantation to overcome whatever spell concealed the bridge.

The shimmer grew into a haze that roiled for a minute or two, bulging and swirling with colors that swam and melted into each other. It gradually formed and settled, finally assuming the shape of a wood bridge spanning the river.

Her horse hesitated at the edge. Riva could hardly blame him for balking. The bridge was narrow, rough, and didn't look terribly sturdy. It was the only way across, however. She would have to brave it.

The span proved sturdier than she expected. It barely swayed or creaked under them as she walked the horse to the other side. The road they'd traveled continued on this side of the river, crossing a short, flat plain, then winding its way into the thick, dark woods ahead.

Before she reached the trees, another surprise popped up on her.

She turned to stare at a bird swooping low off to her left, glittering as it was lit from below by the setting sun. When she looked ahead again, a strange man stood in the middle of the path, only a few horse-lengths ahead. He wore old, almost raggedy clothes in bright and clashing colors.

She halted and stared at him.

"Greetings, Princess Riva," he said. "Welcome to the island."

"Greetings, Good Sir," she replied in kind. "How know you who I am? And who might you be?"

"Fair questions, Lady. I am the Gatekeeper. I have some words for you."

"How know you my name?"

"We know many things here, but of most of those I cannot tell you now. We know why you have come. Therefore, there are things I must warn you about."

"You know my mission?"

He ignored her question. "First, Princess, I reiterate, you are welcome here on the island. There's a cottage not far down the road you will no doubt find convenient for shelter this night. It will serve you in more ways than you expect. Do not hesitate to avail yourself of whatever is offered to you explicitly, but do not, I beg you, try to take what isn't offered."

He grinned and tipped his hat. "I have no doubt such a warning is unnecessary for one such as yourself, but I'm required to give it. There are other warnings as well. First, I must tell you that the island will have many surprises for you, some pleasant, some, perhaps, less so. You'll be tested in a variety of ways. Only those who prove their worth, in their courage, their honesty, their strength, their loyalty, their hope, and their love of others can hope to reach the castle or gain the object of their desire."

"Can you give me some notion of what forms these tests might take?" The horse shied when her hands tightened on the reins.

"Nay, my lady. That, in itself, is part of the test. This I can tell you, however. Harm no one and nothing on the island save it threatens you first. You may defend yourself, but no more. You'll meet many people here, and not all are what they seem. Have a care how you deal with each. Believe not all they tell you. Judge not on appearance alone." He cocked his head at an odd angle. "Do you consider yourself a fair judge of what's in a man's heart?"

"Why would it matter, sir? I thought this was about judging what is in my heart."

"Of course. But is it not so that how you judge others says much about yourself?"

"Possibly. But how can you test such a thing as that?"

The Gatekeeper smiled. "I fear I may not answer you that. But I can offer one final piece of advice. Do you wish to hear it?"

"Why would I not?"

His smile broadened. "My final words to you are these. You must learn not to answer questions with questions."

"I must...? Why?"

But she was speaking to the air. The Gatekeeper was gone, vanished from view between one instant and the next.

Riva waited a few moments to see if he would return. The land around her looked deserted, but when she listened carefully, she could hear in the distance, the sound of voices and possibly music. Finally, she drew a deep breath and nudged the horse into motion. The sun was near the horizon. If she didn't want to spend another uncomfortable night sleeping on the ground, she must find that cottage before nightfall.

Fortunately, it wasn't difficult to locate. No other paths intersected the road she traveled. The wood thickened, with trees growing up right to the edge of the pathway. The trail itself began to narrow, but after ten minutes' journey, it widened again and ran into a much wider, cleared area.

A smooth, carefully kept swath of grass spread over the area, bordered by rows of flowering shrubs and blooming plants. Though she was no expert on flowers, Riva felt sure not all of them were in season. Beyond the gardens and the lawn, a small, wood cottage stood with its back up against the edge of the trees. Ivy and blooming roses climbed up the walls.

After settling her horse, she went to the front door. Though she saw no indication of anyone else in residence, she knocked. When no one answered, she reached for the latch, which clicked open to her touch. The door swung inward.

Riva stepped inside, then stopped on the threshold, startled by what she saw.

Chapter Three

The room she stood in was far larger than should be possible based on the outside dimensions of the cottage. Both broad and deep, it stretched in dim emptiness well away from her. Light filtered in through a series of high windows, windows that couldn't possibly match the position of those she'd seen on the exterior of the structure. A shadowy half-radiance filled the room. The ceiling showed exposed timbers well above, while rich tapestries sewn with threads of gleaming gold, silver, and silk lined the walls.

Silence lay over the long tables and benches that filled the center of the room, a quiet as deep and thick as the layer of dust.

She'd just wanted a sheltered place to spend the night. This looked more like a fairy castle, though a long abandoned and disused one.

Riva moved along the aisle in the center of the room, approaching a dais that supported another table and several padded chairs. Once there, she headed for the most comfortable-looking seat and dropped into it with a sigh of relief.

A soft noise, the sound of a light breeze, swirled around her, though she felt no movement of air. She reached down to the pack she'd let fall beside her when she'd sat down, searching with her hand for a packet of bread-wafers. Another sound—more like the scurrying of a mouse across the floor this time — had her scanning the room for any movement.

Riva saw nothing, but a prickly feeling crawled along her skin. A shuffling, scraping sound suggested other people nearby. She stood up. "Who's there?" she demanded in her most commanding-princess voice. "Come out and show yourself."

The room brightened abruptly as torches set in brackets along the walls lit with flames. Candles in three enormous chandeliers overhead also flared suddenly alight, and wood in the enormous fireplace on one side wall blazed. It warmed the chilly air in the huge hall.

A door in the wall opposite the fireplace opened, and people began to proceed in. Old, young, male, female, all dressed in rich, colorful garments, they marched solemnly into the room in two files that separated at the center aisle. They began to take places at the tables, waiting in respectful silence as the rest of their fellows entered. None of them looked her way or appeared to take note of her presence.

A moment's lull ensued when all were in place, leaving only the other seats at the table on the dais empty.

Another group of people rushed into the room, servants this time, laden with bowls and pitchers and platters of food. Savory aromas of roasted meat and fresh bread filled the room, making her stomach gurgle in anticipation. Other servants laid out cups and trenchers while the food was distributed. Dishes were placed in front of her and at the two empty seats on either side of her by a young man who never once looked directly her way.

The servants disappeared, and still the people waited.

A strange clatter at the door preceded the entry of a group of four men dressed in armor, each supporting one corner of a square platform. On it rested a silver platter, about a foot in diameter, tilted slightly onto one edge, so she could see the swirling pattern incised in its surface. Her heart beat harder when she realized she was quite possibly looking at the object of her quest.

The knights set the wood platform on a set of trestles in the corner of the room, settling it so the platter faced toward the crowd. Then they marched out again.

Still no one spoke or began to eat. Were they waiting for her to start? Riva almost reached for a bowl before she remembered the Gatekeeper's words and let her arm fall to her side again. She wasn't sure if the servants having placed food and drink in front of her truly meant it had been offered.

With another metallic clatter preceding them, the group of knights entered the room again, but in their midst this time marched two others, clad neither in armor nor particularly rich garments. Each wore a plain leather tunic over a white shirt and leather leggings tucked into knee-high boots. One of them was a man, tall, dark-haired, lean and graceful in his movements, his face fine-boned and handsome. The other was — she wasn't sure what the other was. His shape was that of a man, he walked upright, and he wore clothes. In height and size, he was nearly identical to his companion.

But his body was covered with fine, dark fur, the same color as the other man's hair. Shorter fur covered his face, including the broad flat nose, and surrounded an over-large, twisted mouth. His jaw was strangely angled. She couldn't see them clearly, but fur covered his hands as well, and his fingers ended in sharp nails that were more like claws. Other than that, though, his face and general shape were human.

As the two approached the dais, she realized they had the same color eyes, a light, golden brown. Seeing it sent a peculiar, sharp jolt through her stomach.

The knights accompanying them peeled off to the sides, while the two circled the table and joined her behind it, the handsome, human man on her right, the furry creature on her left.

They, at least, acknowledged her presence. Each nodded to her as they approached, and she turned to look from one to the other.

The handsome man spoke to her. "Princess Riva, will you have a seat and join us in our feast? You are a welcome guest here." His words were warm, but the tone and the look in his eyes were cool and remote, bordering on harsh.

The furry man-creature held her chair as she sat back down. She looked around at the others, but no one had yet begun to eat.

"They'll start when you do," the furry one said. His voice was identical to the handsome man's save that his tone was warmer and more friendly.

Riva picked up the fork from the table and reached for the platter of sliced meat. Though none had been obviously watching her, the moment she touched the dish, everyone else in the room began to serve themselves or pour from the pitchers. At the same time, chatter broke out in all corners of the hall.

"Who are they?" she asked her companions at the table once their plates were loaded with food and their cups filled with a fragrant ale.

The handsome man ignored her, eating steadily.

"They are the residents of this isle," the furry man said. "The banquet is in honor of your arrival."

"None of them has said a word to me or even looked at me." She turned to face him.

"In truth, though they celebrate your arrival, you are not quite real to them."

"Am I real to you?"

He met her gaze. Those golden brown eyes were jarringly familiar, even more jarringly human in the furry countenance. "I hope you will be."

"You speak in riddles, sir."

"Nay. I speak truths you do not yet fully grasp."

"Yet are they just as confusing to me."

He smiled. At least she supposed the expression was intended for a smile. "Learning does not come all in a day, Princess," he said. "And you have much yet to learn."

Riva tried to tamp down her annoyance. He was surely right, yet it grated to have to acknowledge it. At home, she was the ultimate authority on most things, and her word was rarely questioned.

"Are you to be my teacher?"

A sudden frown wiped the smile from his face. It made him look particularly fearsome. "In some ways."

"And who might you be? You and your quiet companion?"

"He is Daniel and I am Leinad." He pronounced all three syllables of each name separately, Da-ni-el and Le-in-ad.

Riva thought about the odd-sounding names for a moment before it came to her. "Your names are the reverse of each other."

"Aye." He didn't offer any more information, but turned back to his dinner.

He ate with man-shaped, fur-covered hands, eschewing the knife and fork set beside his plate. His fingers did indeed end in short, sharp claws. Though he didn't use the cutlery, he periodically used the cloth to wipe away juice or sauce from the fur on his face.

On the other side of her, Daniel forked up food from plate to mouth in a steady stream that left him no opening for talking, something he seemed disinclined to do anyway.

Shortly after that conversation, a group of diners rose and went to the side of the room, carrying various musical instruments. Following an unpleasant interlude of screeches and shrieks while they tuned their pieces, the group began a lively round, producing a more pleasing sound.

They played for the next hour or more, while everyone else ate to repletion and lingered over additional cups of ale or tea.

Finally, though, the musicians ended their concert, and people began to file out of the room. There was no ordered procession to the exits. Individuals and small groups rose and departed, apparently when it suited them.

Riva planned to wait until all had left and spread out her bedroll next to the fireplace. Her two companions didn't leave with the others. Even when the hall had emptied but for the three of them, they lingered.

Shortly after the last person had departed, Leinad turned to her and said, "Princess, you are welcome to pass the night here, if you will. Likewise, a bath is being prepared. Would it please you to indulge this evening?"

"A bath?" Even had she wanted to, Riva couldn't have kept the joy from showing on her face. She hadn't had a proper bath in far too long. "Aye, most certainly it would please me."

Daniel and Leinad both rose from their seats. Leinad helped her up from her chair and picked up her pack, hoisting it just as she reached for it herself.

"Come this way." He offered an arm to assist her to step down from the dais, then led the way to a door in the wall behind it. She hadn't noticed its presence before that moment. Daniel followed silently.

They proceeded along a short corridor to the end, where Leinad opened another door to a spacious sleeping chamber. An enormous bed occupied most of one side of the room, its curtains drawn back to show linen and silk covers and a sea of fluffy pillows.

On the other side of the room, a cozy fire drove away the chill. An enormous tub waited on the hearth in front of it. Steam curled upward from the hot water within.

Daniel left the room and returned moments later with a stack of towels and washrags, which he set down near the tub. Leinad tested the water, nodded, and turned to her. "Come, lady. Waste not the hot water."

She looked at them. "Are there no female servants to assist me?"

Leinad shook his head. "Nay, lady, I fear not. Only we two." He nodded at Daniel, who said nothing but didn't look happy about the situation. "I believe you will find we're quite capable. Now, come and remove your gown."

Riva looked from one pair of golden brown eyes to the other. A wave of dizziness, the product, possibly of exhaustion or too much of the excellent ale served with dinner, made her feel light-headed and a bit unreal. The room seemed to swim around her. She remembered her fantasies of the lover who'd taken her prisoner. The lover with those same oddly colored eyes.

"Lady, are you well?" Leinad's tone warmed her with the concern and care it showed.

"Aye. Just...surprised and somewhat overset with wonder. I expected naught of this sort."

"'Tis naught to concern yourself with. We'll not harm you. You are our guest and our responsibility."

Before she knew what was happening, Leinad was helping her out of her over-tunic. The two men guided her to sit on the side of the bed, and Daniel knelt to remove her boots. When he'd stripped off her stockings as well, he stayed in place for a moment, stroking her feet.

Tingles rose from the places where he touched. He rubbed from heel to toe on one foot, splaying his fingers across the top and then the bottom, massaging her instep and caressing her toes. Then he did likewise with the other foot. It felt like heaven, relaxing and exciting at once.

Meanwhile, Leinad had removed her veil and the pins that held her hair up, letting the heavy, wavy mass of it cascade down her back. He ran his fingers through it, gently smoothing and untangling, moving up until he was massaging her scalp. His claws never scratched her, only scraping hard enough over her flesh to bring a relaxing warmth.

Ripples of pleasure surged through her from both her head and feet, meeting somewhere in the middle and stealing her breath.

They remained thus for long, blissful minutes. Riva felt no desire to move or stop them. But after a while, Daniel stood and assisted her to her feet. Together he and Leinad removed her under-robe and then her shift. The fire warmed the room, though she shivered as a breeze blew across her bare flesh. Both men stared at her in wonder for a moment, before Leinad shook off his bemusement.

"Come. Into the tub," Leinad urged. "Waste not the heat of the water."

She thought it would have cooled somewhat while the two men were massaging her, but it seemed it was not so. Leinad and Daniel helped her into water still warm enough to welcome her with nary a hint of chill.

She settled into the tub and stretched out her legs before her, sighing as muscles along her back and hips relaxed in the water's caress.

"It feels wonderful. I haven't bathed in far too long. I'm grateful to you for arranging this."

"'Tis our duty," Daniel said, breaking his long silence.

"And our pleasure," Leinad added.

Both men took washcloths and rubbed them over a cake of soap. Daniel reached into the tub and lifted one of her feet, tenderly running the soapy cloth over it, carefully scrubbing every inch, then working his way up her leg.

Leinad did likewise with her hands, moving up her arms to her shoulders.

It felt like heaven. Her skin tingled and little spurts of pleasure burned into her where they touched. Despite his rough appearance and his claws, Leinad's touch was gentle and careful. Even when he soaped her chest and ran the cloth over her breasts, he never scratched or nicked her. The cloth rasped across her nipples, sending spirals of pleasure working their way through her body, settling in her loins, where something inside began to tighten.

Daniel ran his cloth up the inside of her thighs, nearly to her slit, and she gasped with the delight of it.

Leinad looked her in the eye. "Princess, if we take too many liberties, you have but to say the word to stop it."

She sighed, wondering if she should stop them. She knew nothing of them or their reasons for caring for her. Yet, they'd offered nothing but kindness so far. "You do take liberties. Yet it does not displease me. You need not cease."

What was surely meant to be a grin twisted his lips into an odd contortion, but the satisfaction showed in his eyes. "You will tell us if anything we do distresses you?"

"I shall. Is this normally a part of the island's service to visitors?"

Leinad moved around behind her, stroking claw-tipped fingers through her hair again. Daniel, who'd paused in his ministrations to her legs, answered in his usual cool, almost colorless way. "Few visitors make their way here. Those who do are special in some fashion, and we honor them."

"In this way?" she asked.

"In whatever way seems most appropriate."

As if to forestall more questions, he began to stroke the cloth up and down her legs again. If that was his purpose, he succeeded. The breath caught in Riva's throat as his fingers strayed across her inner thigh.

"Duck your head under the water," Leinad requested. When she'd done so, he worked soap into the mass of her hair and began to massage it to a lather.

Daniel brushed the cloth across her slit. Riva bucked and squealed at the unexpected torrent of pleasure that poured through her.

Leinad reached over and delicately pressed his claw tips against her breasts, sending ripples of exquisite sensation through her. Heat and pressure began to gather in her loins, rousing a need she couldn't define or express.

But then Leinad pulled his hands back and asked her to dip her head again to rinse out the soap. She couldn't suppress a small sob of disappointment. Daniel asked her to stand up. They helped her out and Leinad threw a thick, soft towel around her.

Chapter Four

Leinad read her expression and gave her a smile that showed gentle kindness despite the awkward twist of his lips. "Do not look so dismayed," he said to her. "We've not finished as yet. But the spell holding the water hot is wearing out. We would not have you get chilled."

Daniel wrapped another cloth around her clean hair and then each man took one of her hands to lead her to the bed. Riva went along with them, but she couldn't help wondering why they seemed so eager to do this for her. Who were they? What had they meant when they said serving her was both their duty and their pleasure?

Strange. She'd never felt more like a princess than she did now, with these two caring for her, making her feel things she'd only imagined or dreamt of before. But perhaps this, too, was some kind of dream. If so she preferred not to wake for a long time.

It must be a dream. Man/beast creatures like Leinad existed only in fairy stories and visions. Even Daniel, with his perfect, beautiful features was a creature of dreams, though a different sort of dream from the ones Leinad's like dominated.

Ever since she'd entered the cottage, she felt as though she moved in some fairy space where the reality she knew turned inside out and upside down. Perhaps ever since she'd stepped onto the island.

They urged her to sit on the side of the bed. Daniel massaged her head with the towel until all the excess moisture was blotted up. Leinad dried her feet, legs, hands, and arms. He tenderly wiped away runnels of water spilling down her face and shoulders.

Leinad unwrapped the towel that covered her from breasts to mid-thigh. She looked up at him as he did so and stiffened. She had no idea what this beast/man and his human partner intended to do with her. Both were large and strong. They could certainly force her to their will. Even her small store of magic would likely avail nothing against them, if the magic she'd seen this evening offered any example of what they could call on.

"Nay, Princess," Leinad said. "Worry not. I've already said we'd do naught to harm you. It is our word and bond. We'll do naught you do not wish. Say but the word and we stop. Tell us to leave and we will. Do you wish us to stop now?"

His rich, deep voice washed over her with a suave smoothness, like the swish of finest velvet over her skin.

She shivered, but not from any chill.

"Nay," she answered. "I would not have you stop. Unless you are constrained to this service against your will. That I would not wish to accept."

The two men stared at her in surprise for a moment, then turned to look at each other. Something passed between them. Their frowns turned into smiles, Leinad's a somewhat twisted and misshapen thing that stretched his lips oddly, Daniel's into the first sign of any real emotion she'd seen from him.

Leinad answered again. "Nay, lady, this we do of our own will. The choice was ours. We elected to serve you in this."

"May I ask why?"

"You may ask, lady, but we may not answer. Suffice it that we requested this duty." Leinad moved to forestall further questions, turning her and tipping her backward all in the same motion, so she ended up stretched out on the bed, lying on her back.

Riva reached for the covers to hide her bare body, but Daniel took hold of them and refused to yield to her tug.

"You need not hide yourself from us," Leinad assured her.

"You're beautiful," Daniel added.

"Aye. And we respect beauty, as we respect honor, courage, and loyalty. We pay homage to it in the most fitting way we know." Leinad reached for her but paused with clawed hand in midair. He looked her in the eye. "May we touch you, Princess? May we love you?"

Daniel's hand had already traveled from her shoulder down to her breast, but paused just before reaching the initial curve of that mound. He waited while she considered.

Riva drew a deep breath before she answered. "I have had no lover before. I'm as yet a maiden."

"And so shall you remain," Leinad promised.

"I understand not how that might be."

"Permit us to show you. It would give us pleasure as well."

She stared up into his golden brown eyes. In some ways this reminded her of her favorite fantasy, the dream lover who came to her or took her prisoner. The one with golden brown eyes. She briefly wondered if this was part of her trial. If so, her course was unclear. A test should surely have a clearer path, albeit one that was harder. Yet, she knew little of this island and the ways of it. "Is this a part of my testing?"

Leinad drew a breath. "It is, in a way. Perhaps it would be more accurate to say 'tis preparation for the testing. There is no decision you must make tonight, however. You will not fail or succeed, whether you say aye or nay. For this decision you must consult only your own desires." Seeing that she was still dubious, he added, "I promise that naught you do tonight will cause you to fail. We offer you our services freely because it pleases us and we believe it will please you. In the end it may help you pass some trial, but I can say no more of that."

Could she trust him? Nothing he'd done or said so far gave her reason to doubt him, and she could think of no way in which accepting their offer violated any of the strictures the Gatekeeper had given. "Aye then," she agreed. "Show me what may be."

Daniel knelt beside her on the bed and ran his hand over the side curve of her breast. It sent wild shivers of excitement coursing through her. The tingle of it was strange, unexpected, but delightful. She loosed a long sigh of pleasure.

Leinad stroked a hand down the side of her face. His palm bore no fur, and a hot streak of pleasure radiated from where his flesh met hers. He brushed along her throat and the outer side of her other breast with no touch of claws. When he turned his hand over and caressed her with the furry side, the sensual pleasure of the contact was another revelation.

She moaned softly as she relaxed into the exquisite sensations their touches gave. Their hands roamed all over her body, up and down arms, legs and torso, exploring the curves of throat, hip, thigh, and calves. She had no idea her skin could feel so much, could cause such excitement to gather inside, making her stomach tighten in tension.

Acting almost in unison, Daniel and Leinad each ran a fingertip up the curve of a breast to its tip. When they each pressed lightly on a nipple, the thrilling pleasure of it tore through her like a stroke of lightning. She arched, squirmed, and squealed aloud.

A careful claw tip circled and patted one nipple while a human finger caressed the other. Heat built inside her and pressure began to mount in her loins. Shards of pleasure, almost too intense to bear, ripped through her, going down all the way to her toes, but settling in her loins, where her insides grew tighter.

Daniel leaned over her and ran the same fingertip over her lips, brushing tenderly from side to side. Then he dipped his head toward her and pressed his mouth to hers. She moaned deep in her throat as his tongue brushed across her lips and pushed inside. Another mouth fastened on her nipple, and a tongue probed carefully at the tender flesh there. The combined assault had her writhing on the bed. Sensation, liquid, hot and thrilling, rolled through her, along all her limbs and settling in her belly. It made her cunt swell and moisten. The pressure building in her loins grew to a demanding throb.

Daniel released her lips and licked his way across her cheek to her ear, swirled in the delicate folds there, then nipped and sucked his way down her throat over her collarbone to her breast again, joining Leinad in mouthing her nipples. With lips fastened to each, suckling and stroking, the pleasure of it made her sob and thrash her head from side to side. She reached out and put a hand on the head of each, running her fingers through the silky soft hair and fur. No fantasy she'd ever had could match this reality.

Without lifting their mouths, each extended a hand and stroked her thighs up and down. Their fingers crept to the tender inner skin and brushed higher and higher, until the two sets met at the center of her slit. At first, they rubbed gently, carefully across the outer folds, but then they probed deeper. One set of fingers parted the soft petals and pressed delicately on the inner flesh. She was slick and moist there, and the touch on her clit jolted her with ripples of excitement.

She screamed as a wicked burst of sensation—more pleasure than a body could tolerate—sliced through her. The heat gathered, built, burned inside. Tension drew her into a knot that tightened steadily as fingers—or were they claws?—rubbed her pearl until it throbbed. The combined assault of tongues and lips stroking over nipples, with an occasional sharp nip of teeth adding pleasure/pain, plus hands working her thighs and slit, washed over her, nearly drowning her, lifting her to heights she'd never imagined.

The knot inside her coiled tighter and tighter, pulling her body into a taut arc. Teeth scraped over her nipples, nipped lightly, and tongues soothed the small aches created. Fingers tweaked her clit, pulling and stroking it until the knot suddenly exploded apart, uncoiling in waves of pleasure so sharp it made her scream and buck against the hand that continued to work her. Sparkling lights blazed in her head as the shocks of release jolted her over and over. Her breath came in sharp spasms. She sank into the sea of pleasure and let it carry her. Aftershocks rolled through her for some time, broke over her, making her buck and jolt.

Riva finally lay still, catching her breath. Her body was heavy, peaceful, sated, throbbing with the memory of the pleasure. Daniel and Leinad stretched out on either side of her, their long bodies folded around her, hands still soothing and caressing.

After a while, she reached out in either direction and took a hand of each of them. She squeezed each tight, trying to convey her gratitude. In pressing Leinad's hand, she felt the prick of his claws against her fingertips and was amazed at how gently he'd worked her body. "That was quite…extraordinary."

"Your responses were lovely," Leinad answered. "'Twas a joy to watch."

"Yet, is there not more to this? What of the joining of man and woman? What of your satisfaction?" She released their hands and levered herself up enough to look along one body and then the other. Though both were still clothed, their leggings were tight enough to show clearly the bulges at each groin. "You cannot tell me you have no needs yourselves as I can see 'tis not so."

Leinad brushed a hand down her cheek and turned to kiss her temple. "We promised you would still be a maid after this night. So it shall be."

"It seems not right. I am not so concerned about my maidenhood that I'd see you suffer to preserve it."

"Princess, we thank you for your concern, but this is how it must be. Our choice was made and it stands. The time may come when 'twill be otherwise, but this time we will bear what we must."

"Is there no way you might be relieved without taking my maidenhood in the doing?"

"Aye, Princess, there is, and that, too, may have its time, but not this night." Leinad shifted her a bit, pulling her back down to lie between them. "The rest of this night is for sleep. We are content with things as they are. You may be so as well. Sleep."

* * * * *

Riva woke to see the first light of dawn brightening the room. She was alone in the bed, with sheets twisted around her body. She levered herself up on one elbow to look around. The fire had gone out during the night, but enough warmth remained to keep most of the chill away. Someone had removed the tub while she slept. The clothes she'd worn yesterday lay over a chair, washed and pressed. Fresh linens lay piled on a sideboard beside a pitcher and basin.

She saw no sign of Daniel or Leinad, nor did she hear the sound of any activity. The place seemed almost eerily quiet. Even the bedroom had a feeling of emptiness and long disuse, despite the activities of the previous evening. It reminded her of how the large hall had appeared when she'd first entered the previous day.

Her body protested as she got up. Muscles stretched and overworked the previous evening complained about every movement. Those small twinges had little effect on her overall feeling of well-being, however. She'd been loved—thoroughly, delightfully, and generously—and she was both reinvigorated by it and grateful for it.

She expected to find Daniel and Leinad in the large dining hall, but it was quiet and empty when she got there after dressing and rinsing her face in the basin of water.

The room had returned to the musty, dust-ridden appearance she'd noted when she'd first entered yesterday. Lit only by light streaming in the high windows, it looked as it had when she'd arrived, save for two things, a trencher of food waited on the table at the place she'd occupied yesterday, and the silver platter still rested on the platform in the corner.

She went over to take a closer look at the object of her quest. It wasn't as large as she might have expected, no more than a foot in diameter. Round and flat, it didn't look as though it would be heavy. The pattern incised on the surface showed a group of overlapping circles and squares, while the design circling the border might be writing, though she couldn't decipher any of the words. She touched it with a careful finger, not sure what she expected to happen. Nothing did. It felt cool and metallic to the touch.

Riva sighed and left it where it was. Her stomach rumbled as she caught a whiff of the aroma from the food still steaming on the trencher. She sat down and dug into it.

She'd just put the fifth bite into her mouth when it occurred to her that no one had invited her to eat this time. Her stomach tightened with sudden dread and she dropped the fork. It clattered against the table. She waited for lightning to strike her or a headsman with his axe to appear.

Chapter Five

The air in the place grew denser and heavier. A feeling of dread began to gather around her in a thickening cloud. All she could do was scan the room while she waited for whatever would come.

She expected a thundercloud or a fireball. She didn't expect to suddenly find the Gatekeeper standing beside her.

He stared at her a moment, his face drawn into a grim frown, before he sighed and shook his head. "I see you already realize your failure. I had such high hopes for you. But I feared your background would betray you."

"How so, sir?" she asked.

"Princess, you are so used to being served in all things, 'twas almost inevitable you would come on to something and just assume 'twas meant for you rather than waiting to be invited."

"What happens now?" Despair tightened her throat, making the words sound thin and squeaky.

"Now you must leave us. I regret it, but you must go now under pain of death and never return."

Her heart twisted in her chest, sending a burning ache all through her body. "I understand the justice of it, but I cannot just surrender to this with no effort to change it. Is there no way I can beg for another chance? Naught I can do to show my regret for my error? Or to make amends? I will accept any penalty you deem just."

The Gatekeeper hesitated. "One moment. Let me consult." He was gone in the blink of an eye. No slow vanishing or fading. One moment he was there, the next he was not. She sat down and stared at the plate. The sight of the food repulsed her now. Her stomach roiled and incipient tears burned her eyes. She wouldn't give in to them, however. Princesses didn't cry. But she hated failure, hated the thought of having to go back without the platter, hated letting down her father and all the people of the land who'd been counting on her.

It seemed just moments later that the Gatekeeper returned, appearing as rapidly as he'd disappeared.

"You are fortunate, Princess," he said. "Others were willing to plead for you to be given another chance. At some cost to themselves, I must add." He drew a breath and looked at her. "There is a price to you as well. This will not be easy. Not that it would have been. But 'twill be harder for you now."

"How so?"

The Gatekeeper shook his head. "I may not say. You will learn."

"Is that all?"

"Nay, Princess, 'tis not all. There will be punishment. But of that I can say no more."

Relief poured over her in waves. It mattered not what punishment was meted out, or how difficult her journey would be. She knew only joy that her failure wasn't final.

"I thank you, Gatekeeper. And I thank those who made the decision and those who spoke in my favor. I will not fail again."

His expression didn't move out of its solemn frown. "I trust not. There will be no third chance. And the cost of failure is not borne by you alone. Do not forget." He drew a breath and muttered, more to himself than to her, "Perhaps a reminder… But that is not for me to decide."

He murmured something else to himself, then said louder, "Do not forget," and disappeared.

Riva sat back down in the chair and looked at the plate of food. She pushed it away and rested her arms on the table, then let her head rock forward onto them. Relief that she'd been given this reprieve combined with terror. She'd failed so quickly and so easily. Tripped up by the fact that she was a princess. The Gatekeeper was right. She was used to having people serve her, accustomed to things belonging to her or being provided for her use. It had been that way all her life. It was part of her. How could she possibly ensure she wouldn't fail again?

Despair tempted her to give up the effort and return home. She had no chance to do this thing if it depended on her remembering all the time that she must wait to be offered things. One small slip and it was done. She would surely slip again, no matter how vigilant she tried to be.

The pressure of tears burned her eyes, and she struggled against them. Even if she didn't believe she could succeed, she couldn't give up. Failure would mean her father would have to live with his wound forever, and the kingdom would continue barren and ill-favored.

A small sound from behind roused her. She lifted her head and turned quickly. Daniel and Leinad stood there, watching her. She hadn't heard them approach, but sunk in her despairing misery, she might not have. Their expressions looked harsher, grimmer than she remembered. But then they no doubt knew of her failure.

It took all her courage to meet one gaze and then the other, shamed as she felt by her error.

She sighed. "You know I failed the first test. In truth, I don't know if I can do this. I've been given a reprieve this once, but I must not fail again."

Both watched her with no change of expression. Neither said anything.

"I've disappointed you, have I not? Do you hate me for it?" That sounded pathetic and not at all like her father's daughter, yet she couldn't help it. It burned inside her to think she'd lost the good will of these two.

Leinad answered. "Nay, Princess. We regret what you did, but do not hate you for it. And 'twas not the first test. You passed others yesterday."

She almost sobbed with relief. She might have cried, in truth, but that his tone still held a sternness that unnerved her. "I'm grateful that you don't hate me, and that I passed some tests. But I failed too quickly, nonetheless. Can you help me ensure I will not fail again? I fear my own nature and my life as a princess has not equipped me well for the trials I face here."

Both men's expressions softened slightly, though neither actually smiled. "Aye," Leinad answered. "'Tis a wise recognition on your part. We can help you. But you may decline our assistance when you learn what it entails. 'Twill not be easy, but if you'll put yourself willingly in our hands, I believe we can assist you."

"What would you have me do?"

Leinad continued to watch her for a moment before he sighed heavily. "There are several things, and some you will rebel against as you are a princess. You must give yourself completely to our care, subordinating your own will to our orders and directions. We cannot make the entire journey with you, but if you wish to succeed, you will obey all our commands and follow all our instructions as closely as possible. We will ask you to do things you'll deem unpleasant, foolish, uncomfortable and even impossible. If you agree to our help, you may question, but in the end you must obey."

He searched her face with serious golden brown eyes. "You may say you can do this, but you already know your nature and upbringing will rail against it. You cannot do it in part, either, but only in total. You must agree to submit to us completely, in all things." He paused and watched her, his expression stern and serious. "Do you believe you can do this?"

Had he asked her yesterday, she would have quickly answered that she could do it. After her recent failure, she could not do so as readily. "I know not. This is truly the best way to ensure my success in my quest?"

Leinad looked at Daniel, then back at her. "Princess," he answered. "I truly believe 'tis the *only* way to ensure your success."

She drew a long breath and let it out slowly. "Can you offer some idea of what you might ask of me that I'll find unpleasant or difficult to agree to?"

"Some things we can tell you. Others may not. Some we do not yet know ourselves, but we will require that you agree in advance to follow even those orders we cannot yet tell you of now. First, for your journey, we will order that you go on foot the entire way, though you may take your horse and allow him to carry your supplies. Also, we will take charge of what supplies you may take and what clothing you wear."

"On foot? But that makes no—" She broke off abruptly.

Leinad nodded. "You see the difficulty."

She dipped her head in acknowledgement. "Aye. Is there more you can tell me?"

"Another thing you'll like even less. The Gatekeeper warned that you would be punished for your failure. That punishment is in our hands. We have considered and believe we've found a way to make that punishment serve as a constant reminder to you to be alert and aware of the need to fight your haughty nature. You will be spanked each day, severely enough to ensure you'll be somewhat sore for the rest of the day. The pain will remind you of the need to guard your words and actions."

"Spanked..." She gasped aloud and shook. It felt as though icy cold water had been dumped on her and was running all through her body. Terror sluiced through her veins, yet it was laced through with surprise and a coil of excitement.

Her fantasies... The man with the golden brown eyes. She stared from Leinad to Daniel and back again. They couldn't know... And yet, it was too improbable for a coincidence. She shivered herself back to reality. It might be fun to fantasize about being spanked, but the reality was likely to be much less pleasant. Nonetheless, something in her loins tightened in expectation.

"It might have gone much worse for you," Daniel said.

"But 'twill not be pleasant," Leinad warned. "You must trust us. We may hurt you, but we will not harm you. And 'twill help you to remember."

Silence held the room while she considered.

After a few moments, Leinad prompted, "What say you, Princess?"

She drew a breath and tried to still her frantically pounding heart. "I fear you speak the truth when you say 'tis the only way I may chance to succeed in the quest. I failed so easily once, and I know not how to keep myself from being betrayed by who I am. Your plan terrifies me, yet will I agree to it. I must. I must not fail again."

Both men eyed her sternly. "We cannot guarantee your success even though you do submit to our plan," Leinad warned. "The trials are still yours to pass or fail. This is the best help we can provide to assist you in making the right decisions."

"And I accept it. Much though it pains me to admit it, I need whatever help can be provided."

"You agree to submit yourself to our will and our disciplines?" Leinad asked her in the most formal-sounding tone of voice she'd heard from him.

"I do."

"Very well."

Daniel reached behind him and yanked on the cord of a bell-pull. A gong sounded, then laughter and voices began to drift in from the door through which the crowds had entered the previous evening.

"What is next?" Riva asked.

"A moment," Leinad said, "and you'll see."

Within seconds people began streaming into the room, not in the formal marching order they'd assumed the previous evening, but singly and in small groups at uneven intervals. They took places at the tables again and waited. Unlike the night before, they were definitely aware of her presence. Many eyed her with speculative interest.

A suspicion began to burn inside her, and she had to battle against the urge to change her mind, to run out of the place, flee the island, get away.

Control won out, but not easily.

When the stream of people into the room finally stopped, Leinad turned to her and said, loudly enough for all to hear, using that formal tone, "Princess Riva, you failed a test of the island, but have been granted a reprieve by our intercession for you. To make amends for your failure and to improve your chances of future success, you have agreed to submit yourself to our will and our disciplines. Please confirm your agreement in front of these witnesses."

Her throat felt dry and raspy. It took an effort to say, "I do confirm it."

"Very well. Your discipline begins immediately. Please remove your overtunic."

She nearly protested but was stopped by a look from Leinad. With all eyes in the room on her, she fumbled with the buttons and had difficulty getting her arms out of the sleeves. When she'd placed the overtunic on a chair and stood in her leggings and shirt, Leinad bid her approach him.

He turned so that when she stood in front of him, her back was to the crowd. He reached out and pulled open the cord that held up her leggings, letting them fall down to pool around her ankles. To her considerable surprise, he then drew her against his body, putting both arms around her. He lifted the bottom of the shirt and folded it into the neck, leaving her bare from the middle of her back to just below the knees where the leggings were still caught in the tops of her boots.

Hot color flooded her face as she considered how she must look to everyone in the room. She tried to wiggle away. When Leinad drew her to him more firmly, she buried her hot cheeks against his chest.

"Put your arms around me," he whispered in her ear, "and do not let go until I say you may."

She did as he told her, trying to still the trembling of her body. The situation felt strange and unreal. Nothing like this had ever happened to her. Leinad's hold on her was firm, but not too tight. Almost she could dream it was a lover's embrace that held her. The fine fur on his arms brushed gently and smoothly against her back. Her nose poked into the vest he wore. She breathed in the aroma of leather and Leinad. It was a manly smell, heady and appealing.

But then she glanced to the side. Daniel stood nearby, holding a leather strap that was shorter and broader than a belt. As she watched, he swung his arm back, cocking it for the first strike. She shut her eyes and waited.

Seconds later she heard the ominous *whizz* of leather cleaving the air. Simultaneous with the crack as it smacked against flesh, she felt the shock of impact. It jolted her with a sharp, blasting flash of pain that spread from the center of her bottom, where it had landed, out to every corner of her body. She gasped and clung to Leinad as the area was washed with a deep burn.

Leather cracked on flesh again, making her jump and suck in a sharp breath. It hurt more than she would have guessed, yet she suspected Daniel wasn't striking nearly as hard as he could. She set her teeth, determined to make no sound, to accept her punishment with as much dignity and courage as she could muster.

Five strokes later that effort began to unravel. Her entire derriere felt like one huge, swollen, burning mass. Each additional lash from the strap poured more fire onto it. She struggled to get away, but Leinad held her firmly, refusing to permit her any leeway. She sobbed softly between strokes and squealed when the strap bit into her bottom. But her nipples felt tingly and sensitive from rubbing on Leinad's fur and her clit swelled as well. The fire worked its way deep into her, bringing a tense pressure.

The leather found targets on her exposed back and on the backs of her thighs as well. Somewhere around ten she lost count of the strokes. Vaguely she heard the noise of the crowd watching, murmurs and gasps and an occasional sigh. But mostly she sank deeper and deeper into her own world of misery, drowning in the building fire. Only the comfort of the warm solid body holding her allowed her to bear it without yelling. Nonetheless, that other fire grew, too. Moisture gathered in her pussy and odd shafts of pleasure speared through her, especially when her squirming made her quim rub against Leinad's legs.

The strokes began to bite more deeply, pouring new ribbons of anguish over the grated, sore flesh. She struggled harder to get away or reach back to cover her bottom with her hands, but Leinad wouldn't permit it. Her moans and squeals grew louder, threatening to turn into screams. The sting ran through every nerve of her body until she felt the jolting pain right down to her toes and fingertips.

Control began to slip away. She sobbed and began to plead quietly for it to stop. Yet, she deliberately sought to rub her pussy against Leinad even more as the pressure of need roused and grew. It affected him as well. His engorged cock made a large swollen bulge that pushed into her stomach when she pressed herself against him.

A soft, furry cheek brushed hers and a low, soothing voice crooned in her ear. "You're doing well. I'm proud of you. Hold on, my love. Hold on a little longer. You can do it. You're strong. You're very brave."

Leinad's murmur of support and encouragement continued through the rest of the punishment, even when one very hard blow finally pushed her over the edge and she screamed. Behind her, Daniel cursed. A longer pause ensued, and she began to hope it was done, but then the leather cracked again. It pushed her forward into Leinad's body. Her breasts rubbed deeply into his fur.

Between strokes, she held onto him, moaning and sobbing, and when the leather smacked, she dug her fingers into his fur and muffled her curses and squeals in his chest. Her tears dampened his fur. And through it all, she clung to the sound of his entreaties and endearments. His murmurs held pain and pride and love and admiration. His strong arms secured her with loving bonds. They were sanity and safety amid the conflagration of her body. Need mixed with pain, desire mingled with anguish, overwhelming her into dizziness.

After a while, he said, "Be strong. Just three more and 'tis over."

The stroke that followed was a sharp, hard, intensely burning lash that drove into the tender flesh where her bottom and thighs met. She shrieked her pain into Leinad's chest.

He held her tight and murmured. "It's all right, my love. Courage, now. You're very brave and very strong. Much more than I expected."

The final two strokes were delivered on the same spot, one after another while Leinad continued speaking. "You're a miracle to us, you know. So beautiful as well as clever and courageous."

Blazing pain drove her into a breathless, writhing frenzy.

And then Leinad was whispering to her, "That's all for now. 'Tis over now." She squealed when he let her shirt down and the fabric rasped over burning skin.

Without the strap raining fire on her bottom, she became aware again of her surroundings. A crowd of people had watched. Worse, she was still rubbing herself against Leinad and a stream of moisture from her clit ran down her leg.

He hoisted her into his arms and carried her out of the room, back to the bedroom.

He laid her carefully on the bed, rolling her onto her belly. Daniel came into the room still holding the instrument of her torture. He laid it on the sideboard and joined Leinad beside the bed. He leaned down and ran a gentle hand over her bottom, tracing the paths of a couple of what she assumed must be welts. She cried out when his fingers ran over the sorest area at the junction of bottom and thighs.

"As well she won't be permitted to ride," Daniel remarked. "She could not sit a horse with that."

"Nay," Leinad answered. "And it should serve as a constant reminder to her to consider every action with care."

She looked up at him and met his gaze.

"You'll not sit comfortably at all today," he said. "Yet for all that, 'twas no very severe punishment. There will likely be worse to come."

"I must submit to this—or worse—each day?" Those were the terms of the agreement. "I know not if I can survive much worse."

"You could survive far worse. Be glad you are not called on to do so." They each reached down to touch her again. Flesh and fur smoothed over her derriere, up her back and down her thighs.

There were brief stings when they touched a welt, yet aside from those, the worst of the pain was already fading. No doubt she'd have sore spots, but the overwhelming ache had largely subsided to naught. The desire that had flared in her loins during the punishment, however, had not faded. Each touch made the fire blaze that much stronger. She wanted their touches on the more sensitive spots of her body, as they had caressed her the previous night. It drew a long, low moan of wanting from her and led her to part her legs. "Please," she begged.

Daniel laughed again. "So she is," he said, cryptically.

"Indeed," Leinad agreed, "but now is not the time for it."

Ignoring her blatant invitation, Leinad suddenly drew her upward to her feet. "Get her vest and cloak," he suggested to Daniel. "'Tis past time she set out on her journey again."

The man nodded and left. Leinad drew her upright, helping her to roll over and stand without touching her sore bottom to the bed. She waited, watching him. His face was still just as ugly, with the misshapen nose and mouth, yet she had no doubt any longer that though he might look like a beast, he was a man. The golden brown eyes held warmth and care as he met her gaze. Oddly, she was tempted to throw herself back into his arms. Though he'd been holding her for punishment, she had still felt safe and sheltered in his embrace.

She took his furry paw and held it between her own two hands, avoiding the claws. "Thank you," she said softly.

He started in surprise. "For what, Princess?"

"For helping me through the ordeal. For holding me and giving encouragement."

He shrugged. "'Twas what I needed to do."

"Nonetheless—" Her words were interrupted by the return of Daniel.

"You must be on your way now, Princess," Leinad warned as he helped her dress again. "Time grows short in the day. Daniel has gone through your pack and removed what you may not carry right now. You'll find just enough food for the day and no more. Likewise with water. Consume them wisely. For clothing, you may go as you are, but take no change. Remember, you go on foot. You must not ride the horse."

He led the way out to the main room and across it to the door. Daniel handed the pack to her. She hefted it. Doubts and fear returned when she realized how much lighter it felt.

"Continue to follow the road," Leinad directed. "Though 'tis not the most direct way, 'tis the best. It will take you to the castle. Follow also your sense of honor. Let the soreness of your body remind you to consider well all actions."

"Will I see you again?"

Both men smiled. "Oh, aye. You may not wish to, but for certain, you will see us again. Do not forget what we've told you and stay alert at all times."

"I will," she promised them. "The soreness will surely help me remember."

Leinad stepped forward and folded her in his arms for a moment, giving her a gentle, reassuring squeeze. Riva looked to Daniel to see if he would do the same, but he merely nodded.

She drew a deep breath and stepped out the door, leaving the two men behind. Her horse waited nearby, looking placid and well-fed. She wondered if the animal felt any surprise when, instead of mounting him, she strapped her pack to the saddle and led the way on foot.

* * * * *

She looked back at the cottage as she made her way down the road. It seemed like nothing more than a rough cabin from the outside. She wondered which was reality, the interior or the exterior.

The woods closed in around her again shortly, cutting off the sunlight. A chilly breeze blew. The trip rapidly turned into a strange, lonely journey. The perspective was somehow different when on foot. Noises sounded closer and more immediately threatening, even when it was just birds chirping in the woods or the scrabbling of a small animal in the underbrush nearby. Progress was measured in smaller bits and every milestone took longer to reach.

How long would it take her to reach the castle traveling this way? No more than two or three days, she hoped.

Twice during the morning she caught glimpses of its spires through breaks in the trees. It couldn't be too far away, but for all her walking, she didn't seem to be getting any closer to her goal.

It couldn't really be so, but every now and again, she was sure she heard the distant sound of a pipe, and even, once or twice, the sound of voices and merry laughter. She met no one on the road, however.

Though her feet ached and her entire body grew tired, she allowed herself only a brief stop for lunch. As the afternoon wore on, she began to wonder where she might find shelter for the night. She didn't want to venture too far off the path, but the idea of bedding down out in the open or simply under a tree made her uneasy and was likely to make her quite uncomfortable as well.

Still, as the sun sank lower, she found no likely place to set up camp. She was considering various small clearings when she rounded a bend in the road and faced a foggy cloud not far ahead. It sat low over the road, trees, and underbrush, obscuring her view. She stopped to study it. It looked like a normal fog, save that it had come up so suddenly on an otherwise clear, sunny day. Did she dare go through it? Would she lose her way? Or— She blinked, closed her eyes for a moment, and opened them. No, no mistake.

The fog was moving, rolling toward her.

She backed up a step or two and stopped. It approached much faster than she could back away. Within seconds, the cool mist engulfed her, limiting her vision to only a few feet ahead, surrounding her with a swirling white cloud.

Riva clutched the horse's reins more tightly. If she lost her grip, she might never find him in this. As it was, she could barely see the road beneath her feet. She took a few steps forward and halted. Off to one side, not far away, she heard a cry.

She waited and listened.

A second call, louder this time, was clearly a plea for help. It sounded like a child.

What should she do? The sounds came from somewhere in the woods to her left. If she left the path to go seek the child, she might never find her way back, even without the mist obscuring all landmarks. With the mist, she had no hope of returning to the road. For long moments, she stood still, paralyzed by indecision.

A soft whimper suggested the child was in trouble or pain. Was this a test? Probably — but of what? Compassion or good sense? Good sense told her to ignore it and stay on the road. Compassion argued for going in search of the child. How should she decide? Nothing Leinad or Daniel had told her offered any guidance in making this decision.

In the end, there wasn't really a choice. A series of whimpers and cries made up her mind for her. It might not make sense. It might mean failure, even death. But it wasn't in her to abandon anyone to lonely suffering.

Chapter Six

The horse couldn't go with her into the underbrush where footing was chancy and no trail showed the way. She looped the reins around a tree near the side of the road. Thinking it might be needed, she pulled her pack off and hoisted it on her shoulder. Then she set off into the forest, following the choked cries.

After the first few moments, she found it rough going. No clear path led toward the sounds, and the mist obscured her sight more than a few feet ahead. Thorny shrubs and fallen trees blocked the way, forcing her to go around them. Low-hanging branches tore at her hair, clothes, and exposed skin.

It took her ten minutes to find the source of the sounds in a small clearing.

At one side, in the shadow of a large shrub, a child half-lay, half-sat with his shoulders propped against a tree. His legs were splayed and one of them was caught under the fallen trunk of another tree. She moved closer. The boy was about ten years old. He watched her approach with wary eyes and an expression that varied between hope and despair.

"I won't hurt you," Riva said, wanting to drive the fear from his expression. "I'm here to help. How did you get into this pickle?"

The boy drew a sobbing breath. "I was walking on the log and it...it turned over on my leg."

"Let me look." She moved around to the side to see how badly the leg was trapped and damaged. The tree trunk was about eight inches in diameter and around twelve feet long—not a huge tree, thank heaven, but large enough and heavy enough that he wouldn't be able to lift it off himself unassisted. She bent down to peer under it, fearful of seeing a great deal of blood and possibly mangled flesh and bone. A small trickle of gore had run down to smear the leg of his pants, but not so much as she'd feared. Of course, the bone might still be cracked or broken without piercing the flesh.

"We need to get this off you." She stood up and studied the length and position of the tree. "Let me see if I can lift it."

She went to one end and positioned herself to raise the fallen tree. She expected it to be heavy, and so it was. Too heavy. Her efforts failed to move it at all.

Though she doubted her magical strength was up to the task—manipulation of objects had never been one of her stronger skills—she gave it a try. But after she'd focused her mind on the tree, concentrated her energy, and murmured the words of the spell, the tree remained stubbornly in place. Continued effort to pour her will into the attempt availed nothing.

Finally she sighed and gave up that effort. "I'll have to think of something else."

The child looked ever more distraught.

If only she had her horse, it would be no problem to use him to lift the log. But she doubted she could get to him and bring him back again before full dark, assuming she could find her way back to the path at all. The mist had lightened up a bit, but still surrounded the clearing with a white haze.

Was there anything in her pack that might help? No, but... Riva recalled how a group of men had used a lever to lift heavy rocks from the ground while clearing land for crops. A long branch rested on the ground nearby, along with several flat rocks. She might be able to use them to do something similar. The ground dipped a bit under one end of the fallen tree, allowing room to get something wedged under it.

The boy watched her inspecting rocks. Puzzlement and interest drove out some of the fear in his expression. After looking over several, Riva finally selected one that was the right size and had a relatively flat top. She dragged it into position. Then she pulled the smaller branch over to it, and positioned it under the end of the tree and over the top of the rock.

It took every bit of force she could muster. She pushed down as hard as she could. The tree rose a little. "Can you pull your leg out now?" she asked the boy.

He wiggled and squirmed for several minutes. Sweat ran down Riva's face as she struggled to hold the weight.

"It won't come loose." The boy's voice broke into a sob.

"Hold fast." She adjusted her grip to find a way to exert more force. Nothing she tried seemed to work, until she actually climbed onto the longer end of the lever and sat on it, using the weight of her body to pull it down. Her sore bottom protested, but the fallen tree rose a few more critical inches.

"Can you get loose now?" she asked.

The boy squirmed some more and winced a few times. Riva winced, too, from the growing pain in her derriere, but she refused to give up. After a few more minutes' struggle, he pulled his leg out from under the tree's grip.

She breathed a sigh of relief and climbed off the lever, letting the tree settle back into place. She went over to where the boy still sprawled on the ground, rubbing the leg. "How badly does it hurt?"

He drew a sobbing breath. "Not so bad." The attempt at bravery failed badly, though, betrayed by the tears on his cheeks and the way he winced as he rubbed the injured area.

Riva ran her hands down the leg and found a nasty swelling midway between knee and ankle. She didn't feel any misplacement of bone, however. When she asked him to, the boy was able to wiggle his toes and move his foot.

"I do not think 'tis broken," she said, "but that is an impressive lump you've got. Shall we see if you can stand on it? What is your name?"

"Jerrold, my lady."

With her assistance, he got to his feet. He wobbled a bit, but the leg did appear to hold him up. When he tried to walk, though, it buckled under him after the second step. He would have fallen if Riva hadn't grabbed him around the chest and held him up. In the very dim light, she could see he was pale and sweating. She needed to get him someplace warm. He needed food as well.

She glanced around, noting uneasily how dark it was becoming. "Is your home nearby?"

"Not far," the boy said. "But I be not sure…"

"You can walk? I doubt you can. How long were you trapped there?"

"Since this morning, my lady."

"And have you had aught to eat in that time?"

"Nay."

It was all the food that remained, and it was supposed to be her supper. Riva had deliberately eaten lightly earlier to preserve more for now. But the lack of sustenance would be far more weakening for Jerrold, injured as he was, than it was for her, and she knew not how long it might take them to find his home. She pulled the remaining bread and dried meat from her pack and handed it to the boy. "This should keep you until we can get you home."

She turned and picked him up. He was a small, skinny child, but still a heavy burden.

He protested his ability to walk, but Riva answered, "We'll make faster progress this way. Now, if I only knew how to get back to the road." She set off in the direction she thought she arrived.

"I know these woods well enough," the boy said. "I can direct you back to the road. Go a bit more this way." He pointed toward the left.

He seemed very sure as he gave her directions, and Riva hoped his confidence was justified. When they came out on the road, just a few feet from where she'd tied the horse, Riva breathed a deep sigh of relief.

"Which way to your home?" she asked. The light was fading so rapidly, they'd be stranded in the dark before long. She had a small torch but hesitated to use it until it was necessary.

"Not far that way." The boy pointed at the road ahead.

"We'd best get you there, then." She looked at the horse. She wasn't permitted to ride herself, but she felt sure there would be no harm in allowing the boy to do so. She hoisted him up and walked the horse down the road. The mist had mostly gone now, but twilight made traveling even more hazardous.

Fortunately, as the boy had promised, they'd gone no great distance when they came to a clearing beside the road where several small houses huddled together in a rough semicircle.

He pointed to the second house from the right end. "That one."

Either someone had heard their approach, or they'd been watching for the boy's return. Before Riva and the boy reached the door of the house he'd indicated, it opened, and a woman and man spilled out onto the rough porch.

"Jerrold," the woman cried, running to greet them. "We've been that worried about you. Where have you been?"

The boy addressed the woman as "Mam" and the man as "Da" while he explained about getting caught by the tree and how he'd been rescued.

Riva introduced herself by name without indicating that she was a princess, and accepted their effusive thanks. Jerrold's mother lifted him down and carried him into the house, while his father took charge of her horse, promising they would see him cared for and stabled for the night. At her invitation, Riva followed the mother into their home.

They settled Jerrold onto a lounge in the corner of the room. In the better light of the multiple candles and lamps in the house, the boy's leg showed extensive bruising and swelling. Seeing it, Riva wondered if she'd been wrong in her assessment of the injury. Moments later, the father returned with another woman they called Sharna, apparently a healer. The newcomer set her hands on the leg, closed her eyes, and concentrated. When she opened her eyes again, she said, "Not broken, just badly bruised. I'll give you some poultices and an infusion for the pain. He needs to rest it for a few days, but he'll recover quickly."

Sharna departed, bearing another wave of effusive thanks from the family and seeming to expect nothing more. The boy's parents turned to Riva.

"My lady," the mother said, "we're deeply grateful to you for your rescue of Jerrold. We can ourselves offer you little of food and shelter, but there is a place kept ever ready for guests of the island. 'Tis three houses down — the place is marked with a cloverleaf over the door. You're welcome to spend the night, and partake of whatever food is set on the table for you. There's a decent bed for your use as well. I trust you'll find rest and the fulfillment of all your needs there."

Riva offered her thanks and her wishes for Jerrold's continued welfare, then went in search of the house. The cloverleaf marking was large enough to be easily found, and the door was unlocked.

She wondered what she would find when she entered, and was almost more surprised to find a rough room that appeared entirely compatible with the exterior dimensions of the place. However, as she shut the door behind her, a roaring fire suddenly lit in the fireplace, and candles and lamps scattered around the area ignited abruptly.

To her right, a table occupied the center of that half of the room, surrounded by cabinets, racks, a sink and pump against the walls. On the left, a platform bed dominated the area.

The racks on the right held an abundance of food, bowls of fruit, sacks of flour and meal, even a few loaves of what smelled like fresh-baked bread. The table bore a trencher on which resided a small chunk of bread, a thin, narrow strip of dried meat, and a shriveled apple. It looked highly unappealing compared with the abundance on display.

She dropped her pack and went over to examine the contents of the racks and cabinets. The savory, spicy aroma of a batch of dried meat sticks made her mouth water and stomach rumble. The bread was still warm. She bent to peer at a basket of berries on a lower shelf, but the motion caused a twinge in her rear as a bruise left from the morning's punishment protested. It was enough to remind her. She'd been invited only to partake of what was set on the table. No matter how unappealing that was, or how appetizing the food elsewhere in the room, that was all that was permitted to her.

Sighing, she turned away and went to the table.

Chapter Seven

As she ate the poor fare set out for her, Riva tried to imagine that the fragrance from the loaves on the rack came from the bread she consumed. It didn't truly convince her mouth when the hard, dry bread crunched as she chewed it. Nor did the memory of the savory aroma of the meat sticks make the tough, tasteless strip on the trencher any more satisfying. By the time she'd gotten to the apple, she'd given up trying to fool herself. The apple was soft, grainy, and sour. But the food did help settle her stomach, which had begun to get queasy with emptiness. The cup beside the trencher held a thin, watery, somewhat bitter ale that still helped wash down the dry bread and meat.

Afterward she wondered if she might use the pump to draw water to wash herself, but decided against it. She'd take no chances. Instead, she began to remove her clothes in preparation for going to sleep.

As she dropped the cloak and overtunic onto a chair, a voice behind her said, "You've done well today. We're proud of you."

She whirled to see Leinad and Daniel standing by the table. Leinad wore the twisty expression that was apparently the closest his face could come to a smile. Even Daniel had a glint in his eye.

"How did you get here? Did you follow me?"

Leinad answered. "We belong to the island for now. The island has its ways. More than that I cannot say." He looked at her. "You're no doubt sore and worn out by the day. Undress and let us wash and prepare you." Daniel went and drew a large basin from a rack, then began to pump water into it.

A thrill of excitement and anticipation ran through her. She hesitated only a second before stripping off shirt, boots and leggings. Leinad led her closer to the fire. Daniel brought the basin and cloths. The men each took a washrag and began to rub her down. The water was warmer than she expected, bespelled no doubt, and the cloths soft. They ran over skin with a glide like silk. She shivered and felt moisture gathering at the slit between her legs.

One on either side of her, they began their ablutions at the top, sponging her face and throat, the back of her neck and her shoulders, though they didn't try to wash her hair. Each arm received considerable attention. They washed her hands and wrists, even between her fingers, before going back up her shoulders. Water ran down her front and slid across her breasts just ahead of the first swipe from Daniel's cloth. The gentle rasp of the fabric sent a curl of heat deep into her loins. Then he washed back up the center and drew the cloth slowly, thrillingly over the nipple. She jumped as the contact sent tingles through her entire body.

Leinad began washing her chest on the other side, and soon each nipple was being assaulted by the wash cloths, on and off, over and around, circling into the center, until she was moaning and using a hand on either's shoulder to hold herself up as her legs grew weak. Her breasts were very clean long before the men moved on down to her abdomen, sides and buttocks.

She gasped as the cloth rasped over welts on her bottom that were still a bit raw, but oddly, the discomfort only served to intensify the heat and tension beginning to pull her nerves tight.

"Does it still pain you much?" Leinad asked, putting a finger on a sore place.

"Nay. Only a little. And less when you touch it."

Leinad smiled at her. The strange way his mouth twisted no longer disconcerted her. Now she saw the real warmth behind it, along with the delight that glowed in his eyes. "Did it help at all?"

"It did, much though I hate to admit it."

His kiss was quick, just a brush of his lips over hers, but it still set her heart beating a little faster.

"You're a brave, strong woman. We honor you for it."

The two resumed washing her. They skipped down to her feet and took turns kneeling before her with a knee raised. Daniel steadied her while Leinad raised and washed her left foot, tenderly wiping each inch, even running the cloth around every toe. Then they traded positions so Daniel could work on the right foot.

"I do like the way you honor me." Her words ended in a gasp when one of them reached up to tweak a nipple.

They ran the cloths up her legs, going round and round each. As they climbed to her knee, then up her thighs, the tension grew hotter, tighter. The insides of her thighs were excruciatingly sensitive. Wild surges of pleasure kept riding through her each time the cloths circled over that tender flesh.

When they reached the top, Daniel slid his washrag into her quim and began to wipe it back and forth. She writhed in pleasure and felt herself opening to the touch. At the same time, she moaned and gasped. Just before she would have exploded, they stopped.

Riva sighed in disappointment and turned a pleading look on them. "'Twould not be very honorable to build me up so and stop now."

Leinad smiled and slapped her bottom playfully before he hoisted her into his arms. "Trust us." He carried her to the bed and laid her down on it, on top of the cotton spread. He rolled her until she lay on her belly in the center of the bed and nudged her legs apart.

The feather-stuffed mattress sank as the men climbed onto it, one on either side of her. Hands rested on her shoulders and began to rub in deep circular motions and long straight glides down the muscles. Fingers worked into the tense knots at the top of her back and massaged down her spine to her tailbone. They managed to find all the tight, tense, tired places and worked them until the muscles relaxed.

It wasn't arousing in the same way their sponge bath had been, but it felt wonderful. After a while, she felt as though she floated in some warm space where pain and fear and tension had melted away. They rubbed down her bottom to her legs, still not touching her in an arousing way, but in one calculated to remove the pain of overused limbs. When they worked on her feet, she wondered that anything should be able to feel so good.

After giving her toes, instep and heels a marvelous rubdown, the hands worked their way back up her legs.

The touches changed, working to give her a different kind of pleasure. Fingers glided along her legs and back, lightly this time, sending sizzling tingles running along her skin. The two men worked together so well, never bumping each other or getting in the other's way, it seemed as though they read each other's thoughts. They kneaded her buttocks and stroked the sides of her breasts and the insides of her thighs.

She almost jumped in surprise and pleasure when she felt the touch of warm lips and a seeking tongue on her bottom. Meanwhile, fingers moved up to her quim and stroked gently over the outer lips. She squirmed as jolts of fire coursed through her and the tension gathered in her cunt.

The tongue lapped along the sore spot near the joining of bottom and thighs left from the morning's punishment. The damp coolness soothed and excited her at the same time.

She sighed when the tongue retreated. The bed rocked as the men moved. Leinad lifted her hips enough to allow Daniel to slip a pillow beneath them. When it was in place, Leinad leaned down and kissed the side of her cheek, licked down her throat, and blew in her ear. The brush of fur on her face tingled.

"You're so beautiful," he told her, his voice sounding tense and raspy. "And honorable. So gentle with the boy today, and so compassionate."

"How did you—?"

Her throat closed down and rational thought fled when Leinad reached down and rubbed paws over her bottom, parted the globes, and ran a clawed finger down the channel between them. Meanwhile, Daniel's fingers worked up her thighs to her quim, found her pearl, and began to stroke it. Sensations so strong they were nearly unbearable forced a sob from her.

They stopped for a moment and flipped her over onto her back. Riva could see them now and found it added to her pleasure. She stroked Leinad's ugly face and held onto a furry hand. When Daniel parted her legs wide and knelt between them, she watched him stroke her inner thighs. A surge of tenderness exploded in her along with the ripples of pleasure. He was so handsome. So loving. Hard to believe this was the same man who'd wielded the strap that morning. She hated the pain, and yet even so, it had made her hot.

Daniel found the opening to her womb and explored, working a finger inside. Leinad positioned himself at her side. He leaned over and kissed a breast, lapping a tongue across the nipple, while he took the other nipple between his fingers and caressed. She put a hand on his head, running her fingers through his soft, thick fur while flames licked over and through her. The river of pleasure from the multiple assaults forced moans and sobs from her.

Daniel dipped his head. When his tongue brushed over her clit, she screamed with the jolting thrill of it. She couldn't contain so much excitement and felt close to exploding. He lapped at that most sensitive bit of flesh, surrounding it with his lips and probing with his tongue. The knot wound tighter in her gut. The throbbing pressure grew and grew.

While he sucked on her, he ran a hand down along the slit, from where his mouth still fastened on her bud, over the opening to her womb, until his fingers slid along the edge of her nether hole.

Leinad sucked a nipple into his mouth and scraped his teeth across it. The fire, heat, and pressure of it was a tide, carrying her away, drowning her.

She could hold it no longer. The pleasure burst out of its bounds, streaming over her in an intermittent fountain of jolts. It drew a long scream from her. The men continued to caress her as wave after wave of it broke, carrying her away to a universe where she knew nothing but the ecstasy of the moment and her body's completion. She soaked in it, nearly drowned it, until finally the tide began to retreat. Both men sat up, watching her with satisfied expressions.

When she finally surfaced again, she reached out a hand to either one in thanks. At the same time she realized that it didn't feel complete. There was meant to be more—something to fill her and bring her to the very highest peak possible. And it was meant to be shared.

Because Leinad was closer, she brushed a hand down his body to the bulge showing so clearly beneath the leggings, where his tunic had ridden up. He stopped her hand just before it reached the goal. "Nay, lady," he said. "Not now. The time is not right."

"'Tis not fair," she protested. "You've given me release. I would give you the same, yet you say I may not. I understand it not. This test is mine, yet you've offered me great pleasure. Why may I not do so for you?"

Leinad sighed and looked at Daniel. "Princess," he said, after a moment's pause to consider his words, "Do you think you are the only one being tested?"

Riva sat in silence for a moment, stunned by the words. It had never occurred to her to wonder about them.

Why should it? Then the implications began to filter into her mind.

"Are we then rivals for attaining the silver platter?"

Leinad and Daniel both shook their heads. "Nay," Leinad answered. "Our destinies are intertwined. We succeed or fail in tandem."

"How can we share this prize?" she asked. "For I am sure you had plans for it, did you win, that would not be the same as mine."

"I know not," he admitted. "Yet I believe there will be an answer that satisfies all needs, should we succeed."

"We succeed or fail together," she repeated, trying to absorb that stunning news. "Then if you fail, I do as well?"

"Nay. *You* cannot fail save by your own actions and decisions."

"But should I fail by my actions or decisions, you fail as well."

Leinad hesitated then nodded. "Aye. 'Tis so."

"You put more weight of responsibility on me," she said, sighing over it. "Yet not so much more, I suppose. Already the well-being of an entire kingdom rests on my success."

The beast man put a furry arm around her shoulders. "Do not worry about it overmuch tonight. For today, you have passed all the tests and done well. You shared your meager supper with the boy, and you resisted the temptation to take what was not offered when you arrived here. Now, come and eat well, for I know that poor little bit of food earlier did not suffice. You will need all your strength for the coming trials."

He pointed to the table. The trencher was full again, overflowing with the savory meat and fragrant bread and even a selection of succulent fruits.

"Is it permitted for you to join me?" she asked. "It appears to be more food than I can eat."

"Aye, it is permitted. We'll join you with pleasure."

It was a feast, and they enjoyed it fully, breaking apart the breads and meat sticks to share bits and pieces with each other, slicing up the fruit and passing it around, and feeding morsels to each other, licking fingers and mouths afterward. They made silly jokes about the food and laughed until their sides hurt, even dour Daniel.

When they were done, they all three climbed into bed together. Though she wouldn't have minded a repeat of their earlier attentions, they cuddled together instead and lay quietly. Within moments, she was asleep.

She woke again, not much later, aware that she was now alone. She sat up and looked around the cottage, but the men were no longer there. It appeared they could come and go as they pleased, and by no ordinary means. Sighing, she lay back and was soon asleep again.

Riva dreamed.

It wasn't a pleasant dream.

Chapter Eight

She was in a large room, full of people. She seemed to hover a bit above and to one side of the throng. Most of the people were seated in rows and rows of chairs, but there were five at a table in the front, facing the rest of the crowd. The person in the middle of that group, an elderly woman with abundant, curly gray hair, looked up and met Riva's gaze. The woman nodded, though not necessarily in greeting. No one else took any notice of her. One of the other four at the front table was the Gatekeeper. The others were strangers, another older woman and two men.

A noise sounded behind her. She turned to see four men enter, walking abreast along the broad center aisle toward the table at the front of the room. Daniel and Leinad, wearing long, dark robes that covered them from shoulder to foot, moved in the center, flanked by a pair of guards, each armed with wicked-looking pikes. When they reached the table, the guards moved off to the sides, leaving Daniel and Leinad facing the five at the table. Riva had the distinct impression of prisoners facing a panel of judges.

The gray-haired woman in the center addressed them. "You were assigned as guides for the quester, Princess Riva, who failed one of our tests yesterday. Knowing the price of such a request, you pleaded for her to be given another chance, and it was granted. You're now called on to pay that price. Have you anything to say?"

Leinad stepped forward. "Aye, mistress. We wish to thank the council for their mercy to the quester and ourselves. We pay the price willingly."

"Very well then," the woman answered. "You know what is required."

The curtain behind them slid back, revealing a raised dais about ten feet wide running the width of the room. A bar was fastened to the wall just above head height of a tall man. Sets of leather manacles on chains hung from the bar. A second bar ran parallel to it, just inches above the floor. It, too, had chains hanging to the floor.

The two men stepped up onto the dais and moved back toward the bar. Once there, they each removed the long dark robes, allowing them to drop to the floor. They wore nothing beneath the robes.

Riva's heart clenched and her throat tightened in dread of what she feared was to come.

Guards gathered round Leinad and Daniel, moving them well apart. At the guards' orders, each man reached up and placed his hands on the bar, then waited while manacles were fastened on their wrists and ankles to hold them in place.

Even more shocking, a man came forward with a razor and roughly shaved all the fur from the back of Leinad's body, from his shoulders to his knees. The wielder of the razor took little care in the process, leaving a series of nicks that issued small trickles of blood. Bereft of the fur, his body looked very much like a man's, very much like Daniel's, in fact. Riva's stomach twisted and her hands balled into fists. She wanted to protest, but knew it would do no good and might do harm.

When the shaving was complete, four other men stepped forward. Each was armed with a long, thick strap of some supple material, probably leather. A pair flanked either man, standing behind and on each side. One of each pair held the strap in his right hand, the other in his left. At a nod from the elderly woman, the right-handed ones swung their straps back and brought them smartly forward. Each cracked loudly against flesh and raised immediate welts, Daniel's angling from his left side up across his right shoulder, Leinad's across his lower back. Then the left-handed strap-wielders swung.

They continued to lash in a slow, steady rhythm that went on for a very long time, striking the men everywhere from their shoulders down to their feet. The aim apparently, was to completely cover the flesh with welts. The straps were just broad enough that they didn't cut into the skin except occasionally when an edge struck rather than the flat.

Riva had no idea how many strokes were administered to each. More than a hundred, she was sure, possibly as many as two hundred. It took a long time, and well before it was over, both men bore thick webbings of welts, some blistering and even oozing when further cracks of leather on the same places tore them open, others already beginning to show dark bruises. The only sound either man made was an occasional grunt and a few low gasps. Remembering how she'd squealed and groaned during the far less severe spanking she'd received that morning, Riva felt shamed by their control.

Even more devastating, though, was the knowledge it was her failure they paid for. Just a few minutes into the beatings, she began to protest. "Nay, please, stop it," she yelled. "They're not at fault. Please, no more."

The only one who paid any attention to her cries was the woman in the middle of the head table. She looked up and shook her head. Riva tried to move, desperate to do something to stop what was happening, but found herself frozen in place. Tears overflowed her eyes and ran down her cheek in hot rivulets. She wanted to shut her eyes, but couldn't do that either. She had to watch the men flinch or jump with particularly painful strokes and begin to slump as the prolonged ordeal wore them down.

She couldn't see Leinad's face at all, but Daniel's head was turned enough that she could see his profile. The handsome face was drawn into tense, taut lines. Sweat trickled down one temple. His hair was wet with it and matted on his forehead.

She felt heartsick and horrified at what they suffered on her account. She flinched more sharply with each crack of leather on flesh than they did. Though the straps didn't even touch her, each lash left a bruise on her soul.

Eventually, the gray-haired woman said, "Enough." The straps sank down and trailed on the ground, their wielders clearly tired by the effort. Leinad and Daniel both hung limply in the bonds that held them. Guards stepped forward and released them. Riva was surprised that both men stood on their own when released, but the guards helped support them as they walked out of the room.

The gray-haired woman turned to Riva. Before she could say or do anything, Riva said, "I would speak with you."

The woman nodded and moments later appeared beside Riva.

"Why?" Riva asked. "Why was this permitted? The failure was mine, they had no guilt in it."

"What transpires here is more complex than you know," the woman answered. "They know their role. They knew what they asked and what price would be exacted."

"I would not have had them do this for me."

"You begged the Gatekeeper for another chance after your failure."

"I knew not that this would be the price. I would have paid any price myself, but I would not ask others to shoulder the consequences of my failure."

The woman studied her. "That matters not. The decision was not for you. You must live with it. Such is the way of things."

"Will they be tended now?" Riva asked. "May I go to them?"

"In our normal way of such procedures, they are left to suffer the effects of their punishment until dawn, when all wounds will be healed."

"They suffered for me and I had no say in that. Yet if I could relieve them somewhat now, I would. If there's a price to pay for it, I'll pay it."

The woman had piercing gray eyes. Riva felt as though they could see into her soul. After a moment, her hard stare softened, and she appeared to be debating Riva's request. Finally, she nodded. "So be it. Go to them and give them what relief you may."

"I would request a salve to ease them."

The woman muttered a few low, incomprehensible words. A small jar appeared on her outstretched hands. She handed it to Riva. "Go now." She made a motion with her hand, and Riva found herself suddenly in another room altogether. It didn't occur to her until much later that the woman hadn't said whether there would be a price to pay and what it might be.

Though several torches burned on the wall, the light in this room was much dimmer. As her eyes adjusted, she realized she was in a small cell that held nothing more than two cots. Leinad lay on one, Daniel on the other, both on their bellies, both still nude. Riva moved up the narrow alley between them.

"You are a pair of impossible fools," she told them. "I cannot imagine why you would suffer this for my sake." She reached out on either side of her and clasped a hand of each of them.

Leinad shifted until his face was turned toward her. "Aye. Fools we may be. Yet 'twas not generosity alone that moved us to this. Our own hope of success required it."

"Be that as it may, I've begged a pot of salve to ease your wounds." Seeing them, though, she wondered if she would have the courage to anoint them. It would no doubt cause additional pain as she rubbed the ointment on their welts. Nonetheless, she bent over Leinad, scooped up a blob of ointment with her fingers, and began to smooth it over his shoulders.

He stopped her. "If you please, Princess, see to Daniel first. He isn't as strong as I, and he suffers more."

"Nay," Daniel denied. "This is naught." He levered himself up on one elbow to reinforce his protest, then sank back down with a sighing groan.

Riva did as Leinad requested. Daniel flinched once or twice while she anointed his welts, but for the most part he kept still and silent. For once Leinad seemed disinclined to speak as well. By the time she reached Daniel's hips, the salve seemed to be helping him. He relaxed somewhat as she rubbed, and he seemed more at peace. For her part, Riva found it strange and oddly sensual, despite the injuries, to be touching him this way. She'd never, in fact, put hands on a man in such intimate places, but she found she liked stroking the hard muscles of his shoulders and back, and the gentle curve of his buttocks, even though she remained careful of the numerous bruises and abrasions there. She smoothed the salve over his lean hips and down his long legs.

When she worked the cream into his thighs, she heard his breath catch and apologized for causing him pain.

"Nay, Princess," he answered, still sounding breathless. "'Tis not pain. Your touch works a sort of magic on me. Though pleasant, 'tis difficult to bear."

One or two of the strokes from the straps had worked their way between his legs. She nudged his thighs apart and began to spread the salve there. In the process, her hands brushed against the rough, hairy sacs of his balls. His entire body went stiff and tense, and he struggled to stifle a groan.

"Princess," he moaned, almost pleading. "Let be. You know not what you do to me. 'Tis past bearing."

She did have some idea what her touch was doing. She had no direct experience with a man, but she'd heard others speak of it and she knew what happened. Need welled up inside her, not for her own pleasure or release, but a desire to give to them the same relief they'd granted her. She knew not if it was allowed.

"What exactly are you not permitted to do in intimate relations with myself?" she asked. "I know you're not permitted to take my maidenhead. What more?"

"We may not ask aught of you or accept any… service in recompense for our service to you," Leinad answered, watching with interest as she brushed a gentle hand over Daniel's balls again, making him tense up and moan.

Riva considered his words. "You may not ask…or accept it in recompense. Yet should I desire to offer you…relief, purely as a gift, it would be permitted?"

He hesitated, as though startled by the idea. "I believe it would."

"'Tis good then. Daniel, if you would roll onto your side?"

He complied with her request, not without difficulty, but willingly enough. Riva gasped as she saw him. His cock reared up against his belly, huge, hard, and swollen. She reached out and put a tentative hand on the shaft. Daniel went so abruptly tight and hard it almost brought him up off the cot. But his expression showed sheer bliss.

"I have not done this before," she admitted. "I rely on you to help guide me and tell me if I do it wrong or do something that displeases you."

"Aye," Daniel said, on a whisper of breath. "This is very good now."

She moved her fingers along the shaft, trying the feel of the soft skin over the hard length. When she reached the top and swirled her fingers around the satiny tip, he shut his eyes tightly and groaned. His face looked even more beautiful as he moaned in pleasure.

Riva leaned over and put her lips against his, while maintaining her hold on his cock. She brushed fingers down the shaft and then up again. At the same time, her tongue explored his lips and then dared to push deeper into his mouth. She joyfully breathed in his sighs and moans as her hand pumped up and down, occasionally traveling farther down to cup and caress his balls. He tasted of wine and passion.

She moved her mouth down along his cheek and throat, kissing her way onto his chest. When she got to the masculine nipples, she ran her tongue over each and swirled it against the hard nubs. He let out a long breath that was nearly a sob. The scent of him, something essentially male, comprised of sweat and leather and a spicy exotic aroma she couldn't identify, made her own loins tighten with pleasure.

Riva scraped her teeth over his nipples and stroked his shaft harder and faster.

The throb of imminent release beat against her hand. After a few more strokes along his cock, he panted hard. "Princess, I can't…it's going to…"

With that, he stiffened even more and gave a sharp cry. His cock jerked in her hands, spurting his seed over her fingers and onto his chest. She continued to stroke him until the spasms wore out. He sighed deeply, making his chest puff out, then relax. His face softened into peace as his breathing settled down to a more normal rhythm.

She had to fight back tears as she watched him. Knowing she could give this to him…after what he'd suffered earlier, to see him at peace and pain-free, or nearly so, made her heart expand with a new sort of joy.

He levered himself up a little bit, reached out and took both her hands in his. He felt the stickiness of his spilled seed on her fingers, wiped them along his chest, and pulled her close until she half-lay against him, her cheek pressed against his.

"My thanks, Princess," he whispered in her ear.

After a moment she rose, but before she turned from him, she kissed him again and stroked the hair back from his face. His eyes were soft, his lids heavy. "Sleep now," she suggested, seeing he was nearly there anyway. His head moved in the barest of nods.

She turned to Leinad.

"Princess," he said softly. "You need not..." He couldn't bring himself to name what he wouldn't ask her to do.

"Care for your injuries?" she asked. "There is no question of need. 'Tis what I wish to do. Relax and settle yourself," she told him.

He did so without further protest. Riva began spreading the salve over the bruises and scrapes across his broad shoulders. Again she experienced the raw, sensual pleasure of touching the warm, supple flesh and strong muscles of the man. Even the patchy stubble where he'd been roughly shaved rasped in a pleasing way. Beyond them, fur covered his body, obscuring her view of the flesh itself, but where the hair had been removed, the flesh and form looked nearly identical to Daniel's.

Leinad sighed and began to relax as the ointment eased the pain from his wounds. "You have the most gentle hands, Princess," he said.

"You will tell me should I do aught to discomfort you," she said. "I have little experience of caring for injuries."

"You do well."

She nodded and continued spreading the ointment down his lower back and hips. She couldn't help stroking over his buttocks perhaps a few more times than strictly necessary. Though his flesh was not as smooth and sleek as Daniel's, she still enjoyed the feel of it and the play of strong muscle under the skin.

He flinched, but not from pain, she thought, when she ran her hands down his thighs.

"You tread on dangerous ground," he growled at her.

"There are wounds here." She was appalled by a particularly nasty welt across his thighs where the strap had bit into the same place multiple times. He sucked in a sharp breath as she gently smoothed the ointment over it. His clawed fingers dug into the rough fabric cover of the cot he lay on.

He did relax somewhat when she finished there. She brushed the ointment down along his calves, then moved back up. As she had with Daniel, she nudged his legs apart. A red welt ran up the inside of one thigh, into the fur but visibly continuing right to the bottom of his balls. She spread the ointment over it as well.

He made a sound halfway between a sob and a growl as she continued to stroke there.

"Princess, if you would not begin something you may not wish to pursue, you must leave off now."

"Hush now. Relax and accept my gift."

"You needn't do this."

"Of course not. That's the point. I needn't do so. 'Tis my wish. Never have I had a man so much at my mercy, mine to hold and milk as I would, no less two men. Deny me not this pleasure."

"If thus it is, I wouldn't dream of denying you whatever you would now do."

"My thanks." She brushed her fingers up and down the insides of his thighs. He flinched and moaned when she dared to reach up and brush his balls. Even more daringly, she lingered there, exploring the rough, hairy surface of the sacs. They seemed a remarkable piece of a man to her. Where all other parts were hard and coated with layers of muscle, the sacs were soft and vulnerable. She handled Leinad's with care. She stopped though when he was squirming almost uncontrollably.

"Princess," he begged. "Please."

She put a hand on his side and rolled him a quarter turn, so he lay on his side facing her.

Like Daniel's, his cock appeared huge to her, long, hard and thickly veined, rising from its bed of soft hair. Unlike Daniel's, Leinad's throbbed against a fur-covered belly, though it bore none itself. The fur brushed softly against her fingers when she wrapped them around his length. His face twisted into a grimace that made it even uglier when she stroked up and down. Yet she saw the emotion on his face and sensed the gentle kindness hidden by the sharp features. She watched his eyes scrunch up in pleasure, then smile on her when he was able to relax for a moment.

She gave him little chance to do so, however. She leaned over and kissed him, carefully avoiding the fangs that might scratch or dig in. She moved her mouth down as she'd done with Daniel and stroked his fur with her tongue. His nipples were buried in it, but she ferreted them out, licked, and sucked on them until he was growling and his cock jumped in her hand.

He tasted of the salty sweat he'd earned on her behalf and something so fundamentally Leinad it was like tasting the very essence of the man himself.

Riva increased the speed of her strokes, pumping him, watching his face twist and his body tighten into a taut arc. He gasped for breath and growled softly as she explored the length of his cock. She swirled her fingers around it and up and down again, exploring each small fold and crease, noting what made him groan and squirm.

"Princess, you—" A growling moan cut off the words when she touched the opening at the tip of his cock.

His breath came in short, hard sobs, and his shaft throbbed under her fingers, jumping in faster rhythm. She pumped him until he stiffened abruptly, drawn into unbearable tightness, stretching the moment before he would explode.

He growled long and loud before trailing off as his seed squirted onto the fur of his chest. She kept stroking him until the spasms trailed off and he settled back against the cot with a long sigh.

She tried to straighten up, but Leinad stopped her with a hand on her wrist. He drew her down, bringing her face to his so he could kiss her.

"Your gift is accepted with gratitude and…" He halted and seemed reluctant to go on.

"Gratitude and…?"

"Gratitude and astonishment."

She would swear that wasn't what he'd begun to say at first.

"Think you I'm so selfish, I would not want to give what ease was in my power?"

"Nay, Princess, but I know it must be more difficult to serve me thus, as I have not the beauty of Daniel."

She looked into his golden brown eyes. "You have a sort of beauty," she said, recognizing the deep truth of the words she spoke. "'Tis of the spirit, rather than of the body. You are kind and…loving."

A flare lit in his eyes. "I thank you for that, Princess. 'Tis almost a greater gift than the release you offered and the easing of our pain."

He sighed lightly and she saw exhaustion in his face and bearing.

"Sleep now. Sleep 'til dawn, when I'm told your wounds will be healed."

He nodded, but drew her closer. "Lay with me, if you will, and join me in sleep?"

She settled on the cot beside him. He moved back as far as he could to make room for her on the narrow bed. His arms folded around as he drew her back against his chest. His fur brushed her arms. Warmth flowed over and through her. Peace settled in her heart and soul.

Riva woke to morning sunlight streaming in through the window of the hut where she'd eaten and first fallen asleep the previous night. The delicious aroma of fresh bread permeated the room. Just beyond her line of sight, small noises suggested someone moving around. She sat up.

Daniel was putting wrapped parcels into her pack, while Leinad stood at the table, slicing bread. Both men looked hale and pain-free. If she hadn't dreamed the events of the previous night, it appeared the woman's promise that their wounds would be healed at dawn had come to pass.

Leinad looked over at her. "Rise and eat. You'll need to be off as soon as may be and there are things yet to do."

Riva got up. She reached for her shirt, but found her clothes gone.

"No need to dress yet," Daniel told her.

She nodded and moved to the table, very conscious of her state of undress. Though they'd seen her bare body, she was unused to performing everyday activities such as eating a meal in that condition. It felt odd, humbling, yet freeing at the same time.

They spoke little while she ate. Both men moved with such ease, it was apparent they felt no lasting effects from the punishment they'd endured. That thought reminded her of what she faced. She had to force herself to down the rest of the bread and fruit preserves on the trencher.

When it was done, she stood and faced them. Both were watching her, waiting. Daniel held a long, thin branch in his right hand.

Chapter Nine

"Is there to be an audience for my discipline this time?"

"Nay, Princess. 'Tis not necessary now," Leinad answered.

She didn't ask why it would not be necessary. She suspected they would give her no answer. When Leinad beckoned her toward him, she went. As before, he wrapped his arms around her and drew her body close against his. He pinned her arms to her sides, moderating his strength so that he held her with just enough force to prevent her escape, but not so tightly as to hurt her.

The first stroke of the switch on her bottom made her gasp in surprise as well as pain. It burned in a much sharper, hotter way than the strap had. Remembering how Daniel and Leinad had endured their beatings with such restraint, she resolved to be strong and quiet.

Yet several strokes of the switch tested that resolve almost beyond her ability to endure. Each swish of the branch across her bottom or thighs painted rivers of fire across the flesh. She bit her lip in an effort not to cry out, joined her hands behind Leinad's back, threaded her fingers together to hold him close, and buried her face in his chest.

The burning of her body worked its way deep inside, sending jolts all over each time the switch bit into her. Her derriere sizzled under its fiery kiss. Oddly, though, while it hurt terribly, it again built an excitement and pressure inside her that brought dampness between her legs.

She had no idea how many lashes she endured. More than a dozen, yet less than two dozen, she thought. She jumped with each one and wanted to reach back to guard her flesh and rub away the sting. Leinad held her firmly, permitting only enough movement to let her wiggle a bit and bury her incipient sobs in his chest.

When the pain grew so strong she knew not how she could endure any more without shrieking and crying, he began to murmur words of encouragement to her. He rubbed his soft, furry cheek against hers and whispered to her, "Not many left now. Hold on, my dearest. You can bear it. You have such strength and courage. You're remarkable. Shhh, now. Strength."

A stroke of the branch landed across the welt at the base of her bottom left from yesterday. She just barely held back the scream, but some sound leaked out as a strangled groan. Leinad flinched and he let out a small sob.

"I'm sorry you must endure this," he told her. "Be brave, my beauty. Only a few more to endure. Hmmph." He grunted as another cut landed and she butted hard against him.

Riva was sure the branch must be slicing strips of skin off, it burned so horribly. She sobbed as quietly as she could against Leinad and struggled in his grasp each time the switch landed.

He continued to murmur endearments and encouragement through the final four strokes, though by the end she was squealing and writhing uncontrollably. When the last one landed, harder than any of the others, she screamed and tried to kick out or tear away from him.

Leinad held her until she was calmer and she finally realized no more strokes had fallen for some time. He stroked her hair, combing his claws through it in a way that soothed her while the worst of the stinging faded.

As she quieted, she realized other things as well. She liked the feel of being pressed against Leinad's body. She felt safe with him, secure, and more. She felt loved. And not just due to the impressive erection she could feel straining against the fabric of his leggings. When he finally let her go and stepped away, she wanted to cling to him.

Daniel brought her clothes to her, but before she put them on, Leinad asked her to bend over a chair while he smoothed a soothing cream on the welted flesh. By then the pain had faded anyway. As the switch was falling, she would have sworn it was cutting the skin, but Leinad said it was not so. His paw working the ointment into her bottom roused the heat in her quim again. She spread her legs, inviting further attention, but instead Leinad slapped her lightly. "Nay, not now, Princess. You must be off ere the day gets much older. If you have to deal with an ache of a different sort, that, too, is part of the challenge you face."

She nearly begged him. The pressure of need swelling her cunt was almost as unbearable a pain as the switching had caused. Instead she sighed, straightened and began to dress. Moments later, Daniel handed her pack to her.

Leinad recited a list of reminders. "Stay on the road. 'Twill take you to your goal, though not, perhaps, so quickly as you might wish. You will not be able to ride in any case, but do not attempt it. Remember the Gatekeeper's directions. Take not that which isn't offered to you, and harm no living thing, unless it tries to harm you."

It was nearly mid-morning by the time Riva set out again. With all that had happened in the previous day, added into that morning's switching, she found the walking uncomfortable at first. As she went on, though, some of the soreness and tighter muscles seemed to loosen and the journey became easier for a while.

The sun shone brightly, but trees shaded the way for the most part, screening out just enough of the heat to keep the temperature pleasant.

The road continued on ahead of her with little change. As she walked, she would again occasionally catch glimpses of the castle's spires through breaks in the trees. Despite Leinad's reassurance, she began to worry that she didn't seem to be getting any closer to it. It worried her even more when she realized she was now heading north rather than eastward as had been the case the previous day. The road seemed to be taking her on a rather circuitous approach to her destination.

Just past mid-morning she noticed another of the strange mists approaching. Though its unnatural occurrence still made her nervous, Riva made no attempt to run from it or back away this time. Somehow it was part of the island's atmosphere, possibly part of the way it tested her. Moments later the fog engulfed her in a cloud of damp, cool mist, obscuring the road ahead.

She kept moving, leading the horse, who wasn't happy about the changed conditions. The lack of visibility slowed her progress, however, as she had to make sure she stayed on the road, checked for obstacles, and coaxed the balky horse. Worse yet, within a few moments of the mist's descent, odd things began happening.

Noises swirled through the fog, surrounding her with thin, wispy pipe music, occasional laughter, and snatches of unintelligible conversations between people she couldn't see. It grew louder as she continued to make her way through the white haze. At times the voices sounded so close she should have been able to see the speakers, but never did she catch any glimpse of another person.

That started to concern her when she thought she heard someone call her name. It was very soft, barely noticeable at first, but grew louder as it continued. The voice addressed her as "Princess Riva," and it seemed to be requesting, even pleading, with her to come to it. Sometimes it sounded like Leinad's voice.

When it started begging, she grew tempted to go in search of it. Good sense suggested that was foolish, since unlike the child yesterday, there was no indication of trouble or necessity. The pleas never became any more forceful or urgent, and she continued to resist all calls that would lure her off the road.

Thirty minutes or so later, the mist dissolved, appearing to blow away in a freshening breeze. With it went the sounds of voices and music. She stopped shortly thereafter for a small meal. Leinad and Daniel had given her just a little food for the day, but she'd eaten so well the previous night, she didn't need much.

Both her own and the horse's dispositions improved once the mist was gone, and they made more rapid progress in the early afternoon.

An hour or so past noon, they encountered the next obstacle. If the sunlight hadn't been shining brightly across the road at that particular point, she might have missed it and plowed right on through, but the rays picked out the delicate, lacy sparkle of an enormous spider's web that stretched from one side of the road to the other and loomed well over her head when she stood near it.

As large as it was, though, it wouldn't be hard to sweep aside. She could walk right through it, but she worried about the possibility of a poisonous spider hanging on it. Riva searched the scrubby underbrush just off the road until she found a branch about four feet long, but thin and light. As she bent to pick it up, a sore spot on her rear protested, reminding her of the need to think before she acted. She set the branch back down.

"Do no harm to any creature or any thing on the island," the Gatekeeper had said. Did that include spider webs? Of course it did. "Any creature or any thing." Even if destroying the web wasn't construed as harming the spider, the "any thing" part would presumably include the web. She hauled in a deep breath and let the air out slowly, shaken by how close she'd come to what might well have been a final failure.

But she still had the problem of how to get past the web.

The woods grew right up to the edge of the road on either side, which was why the spider had been able to string the web so neatly across the path. Unfortunately, the underbrush was also extremely thick at that point, forming a nearly impenetrable wall at either side. There would be no easy way to go around it. The web itself was nearly as high as her head—too high to step over.

Ignoring the small stings it caused in her behind, Riva bent down to see how low it went. There was a gap of about a foot between the bottom of the web and the ground. She might just crawl beneath it, but she couldn't get the horse through.

It puzzled and perplexed her. This must be a test— but, of what? And what was she supposed to do here?

She didn't see any way around without damaging the web. She tried the sides again, seeking for a hidden passage through the underbrush or a secret pathway. No obvious path revealed itself, even when she pushed aside thorny branches and thickly leaved limbs. Twenty minutes worth of searching turned up no indications of any break in the shrubbery that would give her a chance to get herself and the horse beyond the web. She retraced her steps, looking for more distant ways that might lead around, but each opening eventually came to a stop at a wall of shrubbery too dense to penetrate or circumvent.

Riva reviewed all the magic spells she knew that might possibly help. Several of them could get her past the web, but all of them would damage or destroy it in the process.

What should she do? Abandon the horse? She couldn't bear the thought of it. But if there was no way around, then the only alternative was to go back. She hated that even more. It seemed like a different kind of failure, a retreat. And it would cost her at least a day of time, possibly more.

She simply couldn't think of anything else to do.

Could she reach the place she'd spent the previous night before dark fell? She didn't know, but without any good alternatives, she decided to make her way back as fast as possible. She turned the horse and began to retreat down the road. It was tempting to mount the animal, especially when she began to doubt she'd make it back before darkness fell, but she'd rather risk the night than failure.

As she walked, other doubts assailed her. Would she be allowed entrance to the cottage again? And even if so, would she be offered food? And what about Leinad and

Daniel? Would they know where to find her? She suspected they would, but—would they be disappointed that she hadn't managed a way around the web?

Perhaps they might give her a clue about how to proceed, even if they were disappointed. At least she hadn't destroyed the web. She didn't think she'd failed. The Gatekeeper hadn't shown up again to let her know about a failure.

The day waned and she grew hungry again. Riva ate sparingly, unsure how long it would take to get back to the cottage. She tried to keep up a rapid pace since she wasn't well prepared for traveling in the dark.

The light began to fade after a while. If only she'd taken more notice of any landmarks along the way, she'd have some idea how close she was. Occasional glimpses of the castle towers continued to tease her. They might serve as landmarks, too, but since she barely remembered where she'd been when she'd seen them earlier, that wasn't much help.

Mercifully she didn't encounter any mists to slow her along the way. Even so, she tried to travel even faster, despite the hunger beginning to gnaw at her stomach, which growled and roared periodic pleas for sustenance. The light dimmed by the minute.

Chapter Ten

Twilight had deepened almost to night when she finally rounded a curve and saw the small group of homes clustered in a semicircle some ways ahead.

Breathing a sigh of relief, she urged the horse forward. For the last few hundred yards, they moved in near-complete darkness, and she tread carefully for fear of stepping into an unseen hole or obstacle.

Relief rolled over her in waves when she noted the light shining in the windows of the cabin, until it occurred to her that there might be another guest or quester occupying the place. Would they be willing to share? Actually she hoped there wasn't another guest, but since that wasn't a worthy thought, she refused to dwell on it.

She left her horse out front while she knocked on the door. It swung open, but no one appeared in the entrance to greet her. Nor did there appear to be anyone else present, despite the fire in the grate and the burning lamps on various shelves. A plate of food waited on the table.

Riva was so hungry, she nearly went and gobbled it down. Just in time, she remembered that no one had offered the food to her. For that matter, the shelter of the cabin hadn't been offered either, unless the door opening by itself constituted such. Her instincts said it was, but she still hesitated to remain.

"You are welcome to pass the night here and partake of the food."

Leinad's voice came from behind her, making her jump in surprise. Odd, how she never saw either he or Daniel coming or going. One minute they weren't there, the next they were. Always behind her, it seemed, or while she was asleep or looking the other way.

"How do you do that?" she asked.

"Do what?"

"Come and go without my seeing you."

Leinad's face twisted into that strange grimace that was the nearest he could come to a smile. "We are part of the plan."

"That doesn't answer my question."

"No, but 'tis all I may tell you."

"I see." She stared at him a minute, wondering if he knew of her failure already. Since he and Daniel were here, she had to assume he did. There was something immensely reassuring, nonetheless, about their presence. And something more, beyond reassuring, beyond even the sexual excitement the memories of their activities the previous couple of evenings brought, or the tingle of fear their discipline inspired.

She wouldn't have believed she could think of them as friends. Yet she was glad to see them, and not just for the reassurance they represented. Despite his ugly face, Leinad had a warm heart and a streak of tenderness. He seemed to genuinely care about her and her welfare. Daniel was more enigmatic, but despite his dour and reserved demeanor, he appealed to her in ways beyond the physical beauty of his face and body. They'd certainly made a tremendous sacrifice to give her another chance, though Leinad had suggested it was in their own interest to do so as well. She wanted their good regard and hated that she might disappoint them.

She sat in the chair at the table, letting her shoulders sag with her exhaustion and depression. "As you are here, I suppose you must know that I failed one of today's tests. Or at least, I failed to pass it. Since the Gatekeeper hasn't come to pronounce my doom, I conclude I didn't fail completely. I certainly didn't pass."

Leinad came to her and knelt on the floor beside her. He reached out a paw and brushed it down her cheek, careful to keep his claws off her skin.

"You did not fail today, Princess. You passed the test."

She looked up at him, startled. "I could not find a way around the spider web."

"You were not supposed to. The only ways you could have gone on would have meant either abandoning your horse or destroying the web. Either of those would have been a failure."

"But I had to turn back, and I've now lost an entire day."

"And what does a day of your time matter compared to that spider's lifetime work?"

That stopped her for a moment. She'd never considered such a thing. She was a princess, and always her time had counted as more important than anyone else's. To be considered less important than a spider…achieving her goal would save her entire land as well as her father. Leinad was correct that a day extra would hardly make any great difference. But…

"It will still be there tomorrow when I take to the road. How can I get around it to continue with my journey?"

"It will not be there tomorrow. You will be able to go on. There will be other obstacles, of course."

"The correct action was to give up and turn back around?"

"It was. Forging ahead through any and all obstacles isn't always the proper way to get to your goals."

"That seems an odd thing, yet I see how it might be so." She thought about other instances she knew of where the quickest and easiest way wasn't always correct, and retreat not always a failure. "When an army meets a far superior foe, 'tis wiser to retreat and find more support before facing the enemy."

Leinad nodded. "And at times respect for another's life or living compels one to alter one's own plans."

"Aye. Some time ago we wanted to divert a creek to provide more water for our own cattle, yet didn't do so, as it would have taken water the miller needed to run his wheel."

Leinad nodded and stared at her for a moment. Riva watched his eyes as well. Strange how warmly human they were, even in that ugly, furry face. How very attractive. Even more so than Daniel's despite his beautiful face. She had no idea why it should be so.

Leinad put his arms around and hugged her to his leather-clad shoulder for a moment before he stood up again. "You're exhausted and hungry. Eat now. You're welcome to partake of what is here."

She nodded and turned back to the table. The trencher before her now bore a load of appetizing foods, roasted meat, fresh, warm bread, a fruit compote and roasted tubers, sprinkled with herbs.

Instead of the party-like way they'd attacked the food the previous night, this evening the three of them ate mostly in silence. Riva was too exhausted to do more than fork up the food and struggle to keep from falling asleep right there. Toward the end of the meal, she began to lose the battle.

She wasn't even aware she'd dozed off until she felt a pair of strong arms lifting her from the chair. She blinked and looked up at Leinad. He carried her to the bed and set her down. He looked like a large, furry cat to her sleep-befogged eyes, one she would like to have hold and cuddle her. But she couldn't stay awake long enough even to ask.

She dreamed again that night, but this one was much more a dream than the previous night's experience.

Her dream-lover—the one she had fantasized about for years—came to her, wearing the usual enveloping dark clothes and mask concealing his features. The only really distinct feature she could discern were the eyes, that remarkable, wonderful, warm golden brown color.

She was his prisoner, kidnapped for reasons unknown, and kept locked in a tower room. Her quarters bore little other resemblance to a dungeon, however, as they included an extravagant and very comfortable bed with feather-stuffed mattress and pillows, and linen bedclothes with gold embroidery. A large chifforobe occupied one corner of the room, and while the doors were closed, she knew it contained a variety of rich and beautiful clothes, all sized to fit her.

Still, she was a prisoner and felt it her duty to try to escape. The fantasy proceeded along its normal lines. She tried to run away after she somehow pushed or shoved and caused him to lose his balance. But he caught up with her before she'd gone far, carried her back to her quarters, turned her over his knee, and spanked her for the attempt. Spanked her for a long time, hard enough to hurt considerably and make her cry and beg him to stop.

Yet at the same time the burning ache worked its way from her derriere deep into her loins, extending to her quim, which began to swell with excitement and throb with need.

By the time he finished, she was sobbing, though more from the overwhelming mix of emotions than from pain. When he set her upright again and drew her into his arms, she clung to him. Her tears flowed freely, dampening his shirt. His arms tightened around her, and his fur brushed her cheeks.

She needed him so badly.

In her dream, he growled into her ear, "I've waited long enough, and done all in my power to gain your willing acceptance. Now I'll have you whether you will it or not."

"My father will kill you for it, should he find out."

"I'll take the risk. Now, my dear…" He tipped her face up so her eyes met his. "Will I truly have to force you? I would prefer not to."

She drew a deep breath, acknowledging to herself she no longer had the power to resist him and the feelings he roused in her. "Nay, my lord, you'll not have to force me. In truth, you've long had my love, but I feared for your life should you do this thing and my father learned of it. I need you too much. I will take you willingly enough, even eagerly."

"My love," he said, bringing his face down and kissing her until her head was reeling with the sweetness of it. It stoked the fire already burning in her loins until she could bear the pressure no longer.

He stood her in front of him and rapidly removed her clothes, then he laid her reverently on the bed. He stroked her breasts and her thighs until she was sobbing and gasping for him.

He shucked off his own clothes. She couldn't see his body clearly, though the outline of it was graceful and attractive. His cock stood out proudly, long and hard. He positioned himself over her, but fingered her slit to test the moisture gathered there.

"Are you ready, my love?"

"Come into me," she begged.

With a hard thrust, he pushed his way in.

It filled her with its heat and strength.

She gasped.

He withdrew a bit and then pushed in again, even further.

"Ah, lord, it feels so good," she moaned. "Give me all of you, if you please. I need it all."

"My beauty." He kissed her deeply yet again. "All I have to give is yours."

On the next thrust, he buried himself completely in her. His hard cock touched something within that roused a fierce pleasure and knotted her insides tightly.

He withdrew a bit and plunged again. Several more times, and he was gasping as hard as she. Then he buried himself, withdrew, and waited for a moment that seemed endless. With a roar, he rammed himself home in her yet again and his hot seed spurted into her.

At the same time, she felt the knot tying up her gut suddenly spring loose, releasing her in a series of ecstatic spasms that made her shiver and buck.

They both shook with the force of their release for some time. Once they'd calmed, he lowered himself so he lay completely on top of her for a moment, then rolled to her side. He gathered her close in his arms and held her securely as he murmured endearments, telling her how wonderful she was, how beautiful, how warm and loving, how much he loved her. He said he would have her for his wife, no matter how many objections others would raise.

She agreed to be his, even if they had to fight the entire world for the right to be together.

As she faded back into sleep, a shiver of dread passed through her. She would have to fight for him, she knew, and it was going to cost her a great deal.

Chapter Eleven

She woke in the morning to find herself sandwiched between Daniel and Leinad in the bed. Daniel's hand cupped her breast, while Leinad's paw rested on her thigh. When she roused and moved, they each withdrew the touch. It disappointed her. The dream had left her feeling heavy, needy, almost pulsing with desire. She wanted to drag them to her and ask them to give her release.

They didn't offer it though. Instead each rolled off the bed and walked away. She got up as well.

In most respects, that morning was a repeat of the previous morning. Again her clothes were missing and she took breakfast in the nude. After the meal, they punished her again.

It was done a bit differently that morning. Before it began, Leinad warned that she would receive just a few strokes, but they'd be harsher than those she'd had before. Then he turned his back to her and told her to put her arms on his shoulders. When she did so, he took hold of her wrists and drew up until her feet were off the floor. He leaned forward, holding her wrists firmly. Her breasts were crushed against his back, her head lying on his shoulder, her legs dangling freely.

"Are you ready?" Daniel asked. She couldn't tell whether the question was addressed to her or to Leinad.

The latter answered, "Aye."

She couldn't have done so, in any case. She wasn't ready. She'd never be ready. Yet her cunt throbbed with combined excitement and dread.

Because her head was twisted away as it rested on Leinad's shoulder, she couldn't see Daniel at all and had no idea what he held.

An ominous swish preceded a loud crack when something solid and horrible crashed into her bottom. A fierce, fiery pain, deeper and harsher than anything she'd felt before, tore across her derriere. It drew a strangled scream from her. She kicked and writhed, trying to tear herself out of Leinad's grip, desperate to avoid another stroke.

It didn't work, of course. The next cut fell a bit lower and burned like hundreds of bees stinging. She buried her face in Leinad's shoulder as she wriggled. But as before the pain roused something else when the burn worked its way deep into her. Her quim swelled and got moist as it banged against Leinad's backside.

On the third stroke, she squealed and kicked at Leinad, struggling at first to get away, but then to rub herself against him hard enough to send the lightning bolts of sharp pleasure through her.

"Easy," Leinad said, trying to soothe her. "Not much more. Be brave, my dear."

Still, by the fifth stroke, Riva was beyond being brave or controlled or dignified. She screamed, kicked, and begged for them to stop. In between she rubbed her quim frantically against him. She barely heard when Daniel said, "Just one more."

The "one more" was a powerful stroke that seared into her bottom with such painful intensity, it sent her into a frenzy. She scratched at Leinad with her fingernails and kicked him so hard it had to leave bruises. She heaved up and down, moaning and squealing. Her derriere was on fire, burning up, so hot and stinging, she couldn't bear it.

While she was still wiggling, Leinad let her down and turned quickly so he caught her before she collapsed to the floor. He gathered her into his arms and cuddled her close to him, letting her sob against his shoulder. He whispered words of encouragement and admiration in her ear while she recovered her composure. As much as her bottom hurt, she could still appreciate how nice it felt to be held against him, to have his arms around her, holding and protecting her. Even more, though, she needed his touch on her clit.

Riva was surprised when Daniel came and stood nearby, then put a hand on her arm to draw her attention.

"I'm sorry," he said. "'Twas harsh. I'm sorry I had to hurt you so much."

Leinad looked at Daniel and said, "You have naught to apologize for. 'Twas necessary. Riva knows that. She may not like it, but she knows the discipline is helping her to remember." He looked down at her. "Is it not?"

With her bottom still burning, she hated to admit it. But he was right and she owed them her honesty. "Aye, 'tis helping."

Leinad nodded. "Come, lie down a moment," he said, drawing her to the bed.

Daniel approached with a pot of salve. Leinad brushed a careful hand over her bottom. "You have some nice welts here," he told her. "They'll be sore for a while." He bent down and kissed along the line of one of the marks. The touch of his lips on those raw places stung, yet at the same time, it added to the explosive pressure of need inside her. She moaned and parted her legs, begging them to touch her and give her release.

Leinad smoothed some of the ointment over the sore welts, but he carefully avoided getting close to her slit, denying her the touches she desperately wanted.

She parted her legs and begged. "Please. I need...oh, please!"

When a hand moved into the cleft between her legs and fingers sought her pearl, she almost sobbed with joy.

She needed it so badly after the powerful stimulus of the punishment.

She was so aroused it took only a few strokes of the fingers over her quim to make her come in giant, heaving spasms.

One of the men continued to stroke her thighs and cleft while the other kissed her bottom and up along her back to her neck, until she finally calmed.

She sank into a light doze that ended quickly when the bed rocked as the two men moved.

"You need to be on your way," Daniel said to her.

Leinad offered a hand and helped her up off the bed. It was painful to put her leggings on. The material rubbed over her welts. Walking was difficult as well since every movement made the lines on her bottom burn.

Still, it was part of the trial, what she needed to bear to get to her goal.

Before she set out again, Leinad offered the usual set of warnings about staying on the road, thinking before she acted, and doing no harm. "There are shorter, quicker ways to get to the castle, but they will lead ultimately to your failure," he warned, and added, "You must follow this road all the way. Do not fear to act when it is needed or to defend yourself when attacked. Take care that you understand the difference."

She mused on that bit of advice for the first hour or so of her journey. Would it not be obvious when she needed to defend herself?

Somewhat to her amazement, the fierce soreness in her bottom subsided quickly, though she still felt it when she moved in certain ways. She couldn't possibly ride the horse, which removed one temptation.

The road still bore northward, although it seemed to bend toward the west as she continued on it.

She met the first obstacle—or test—shortly after midmorning. A series of anthills pocked the road for several hundred yards. They hadn't been there the previous day, but she was learning that things were rarely what they seemed on this island, and reality could change at a moment or a thought.

Riva studied the piles of dirt. In another time and another place, she would still have been cautious about them as ant stings were no fun, but she would likely have let her horse plough on through, careless of the havoc. Now she considered it a necessity that she find a way past them without damaging the mounds.

She noted the spacing of the hills. If she were to weave her way through by stepping in one spot, then in the next clear one, she could manage. It would take a great deal of care to get the horse through without him kicking or stepping on one, but it could be done.

Moving with delicate precision, she guided the horse through the maze of anthills, watching all the time where each hoof would land. She frequently had to nudge or turn him to prevent him putting a foot in the wrong place. The horse wasn't thrilled about it and occasionally balked. It took every bit of horse-skill she possessed to get him through that course. At the same time, she had to keep watch where she put her own feet.

For the last few yards of it, the hills were closer together, making it even more difficult to negotiate. Though it galled her to take so much time, every twinge of her bottom as she twisted and turned herself or pushed and prodded the horse reminded her of the need for caution. Fighting her own impatience, she proceeded carefully until she and the horse finally cleared the last of the anthills.

For a while the road leveled out again and the way became smooth. She walked faster, hoping to make up for some of the time lost on the anthills.

They had only a short break before they reached the next obstacle. A pack of foxes crossed the road ahead. Riva stopped well in advance and let them pass, hoping it wouldn't take them long. Though she thought it unlikely they'd attack, she drew her sword from the sheath strapped to the saddle, and held it ready while she waited.

The group seemed in no hurry to get to the other side, though. When she tried to push ahead, a couple of the animals faced her and growled. She got the message and backed away again. The wait until the entire group had crossed the road and ambled off into the shrubbery stretched her patience nearly to the breaking point.

Once the foxes had finished their leisurely passage and disappeared, she resheathed the sword and set out again. By midmorning the sun was almost directly behind her as the road turned more clearly westward. She caught one glimpse of the castle's spires off to her left and judged she was still no nearer. It appeared the road was circling around her destination. She wondered how far around it would go before she got any closer.

Not long after that glimpse of the castle, she heard a series of snuffles and growls ahead. It took a few more minutes before she could discern what formed the bunch of animals that partly blocked the road. Dogs. At least twenty of them, in various sizes, colors, and breeds. A few of them fought, snarling and snapping at each other. Most of them patrolled the road, as if guarding it against the passage of any other creatures.

Riva halted, drew a deep breath, and pulled out the sword again. For almost the first time, she felt real, physical fear. She'd never liked dogs and had always been a bit afraid of them. She avoided her father's and brother's hunting hounds, and wasn't even very fond of her sister's lap dog, fat, placid ball of fur that he was.

No fat or placid creatures these, though. They were lean, tense, and snarlingly alert. She had no idea how to get past them.

The trees and shrubbery grew densely up to the edge of the road. A detour would cost her hours and risk injury to the horse. She could invite the dogs to attack her, and thus use the sword to defend herself, but the pack was large enough to make her doubt she could win such a battle.

They didn't completely block the road, but she suspected they would move into her path if she attempted to go forward. To test the theory, she took two careful steps forward. The dogs' ears all twitched, the hairs on their necks rose, and they moved toward her.

Chapter Twelve

Riva halted and backed up hastily, waving the sword to ward off any lunges. The dogs stilled, but most continued to watch her with hot, hungry eyes.

There were too many of them to fight, and they wouldn't just let her pass.

Cold chills slithered up and down her spine. She didn't want to get near them, much less go past. Was she supposed to give up and go back again? Probably not. Even if she couldn't get around them, they could move out of the way. There should be a way past without harming them. Unless they attacked. She wasn't sure what she'd do if they attacked.

She eyed them as she considered the issue. They looked mean and hungry.

Hungry.

Riva considered the food she carried with her. Daniel had put more than usual into her pack. She'd thought he'd done so because she'd eaten less breakfast, but perhaps there had been another reason.

Moving slowly and carefully to avoid startling the milling group of animals, she transferred the sword to her left hand, reached into her pack with her right, and withdrew a packet of cheese.

The animals must have smelled the food. Several of them turned toward her and began to advance. She went cold from head to foot with terror, hastily broke off a piece of the cheese, and tossed it as far as she could into the woods on the left. All but three of the dogs took off in pursuit. She couldn't see them, but an interlude of growling and snarling from the group made her shiver. All too quickly, they came running back, and this time they moved closer, eyeing the remaining cheese she held.

Out of time for planning, Riva took the remaining cheese, crumbled it in her hand, and tossed it again, throwing as hard as she could, hoping the bits would spread out and lure the animals into searching for them.

The dogs took off, leaving only one behind this time. Riva transferred the sword back to her right hand, grabbed the horse's reins, and ran forward. Ferocious snapping, growling, and snarling told her the dogs were finding— and fighting over—the bits of cheese. The temptation to jump on the horse's back nearly overwhelmed her. It took a huge effort to resist.

She eyed the one remaining dog as she approached. It didn't look too ferocious, but she didn't trust appearances. She kept the sword ready.

The animal watched her as she ran past. It didn't show any sign of attacking. In fact, it looked lost, hungry, and hopeful.

From off to her right, though, the rest of the group was returning. Riva reached into her pack and found a chunk of bread, crushed it, and threw it. The dogs turned again and chased after the food. All except for the one that remained, watching her with that longing expression.

He had to be hungry, but he was neither fighting the others for food, nor attacking her. She didn't understand it, but something about the way the dog waited, tail wagging, touched her. She grabbed the last piece of bread in her pack, all that remained of her lunch, and tossed it at the creature.

The dog leapt for the chunk of bread, then looked up at her with the piece clenched between its teeth. Before it ran off, its tail waved back and forth a couple of times, and she could almost swear it grinned at her.

She turned and ran, wanting to put as much distance as possible between herself and the rest of the pack. She worried they might try to follow and even catch up with her.

The sounds of the dogs' snarling and fighting retreated into the distance. She didn't hear it again, but it was still a while before she began to relax.

She reached a place where there were fewer trees along the roadside, though the underbrush remained thick. The sun beat on her relentlessly and sweat began to trickle down her temples, along her spine, and between her breasts.

Shortly after mid-day she encountered another mist. Again, she heard the noises of people laughing and talking. At times she thought someone called to her, but she met no one.

Until she rounded a bend, emerged from the mist, and saw a man sitting in a small clearing beside the road. He rested on a colorful, woven blanket he'd spread on the grass. A basket sat nearby.

"Greetings, Princess," he called to her as she approached. "Would you join me for some lunch?"

She debated about the offer. All her food had gone to the dogs, and her stomach rumbled loudly. Daniel and Leinad hadn't said anything about accepting food from a stranger, and he was offering it to her. In any case, it would surely be rude to refuse his generosity.

"Aye, sir, with thanks." Riva fastened the horse's reins to a nearby tree and joined the man at the blanket.

"Please, have a seat," he answered. "I've bread, some berry preserves, roasted fowl, and a nice wine. May I serve you?"

"Aye, thank you, sir. I'm Princess Riva," she told him, "though clearly you already know that. Who might you be?"

"Your pardon, Princess. I'm called Varek." He handed her a chunk of meat wrapped in a slice of bread.

Riva stared at him for a moment. He was a handsome man, probably only a few years older than herself, with blond hair and eyes as blue as the sky on a clear spring day. He wore a shirt of fine lawn, embroidered at the throat and sleeves, over leggings of blue silk. An overtunic of deep green silk lay nearby.

He poured two cups of wine before he lifted his own meat roll and took a bite. That was when he noticed she wasn't eating. "Please." He gestured for her to put food in her mouth.

She shook herself and took a bite, chewing slowly to enjoy the taste. The meat was savory, the bread soft and fresh. "This is wonderful."

"Aye. My cook has a way with food. I think you'll enjoy the wine as well. It's from a very good year."

They each picked up a cup and sipped at it. It was very likely the best wine she'd ever tasted, rich, smooth, and fragrant with a woodsy aroma. While they ate, he asked her about herself, drawing her to talk about her family and their lands until the meal was done.

He poured more wine and they drank deeply. The warmth of the day, the satisfaction of a full belly, and the soothing effects of the wine combined to make her feel very sleepy. Her eyelids grew heavy and she began to doze.

As she lay back down, though, she pressed one of the welts from earlier to the ground. The ache reminded her that she needed to continue on her journey. She had no idea where she'd be spending that night, but she somehow knew she needed to keep going and cover as much ground as she could that day.

So she roused herself and shook off the lethargy. "I thank you for the meal, sir," she told Varek. "Your food was wonderful. And I thoroughly enjoyed it, but I have some distance yet to cover today, so I must needs be underway again. I trust we'll meet again."

He smiled at her. "I believe we will, Princess, and I look forward to it. I should like to get to know you better." Something sensual in his tone and look promised carnal delights beyond those provided by the food and wine.

"I shall look forward to it." She unwound the horse's reins and led him out of the clearing. "My thanks again for the food," she called as she walked away from Varek.

The next hour or so was a continual struggle to stay awake and keep moving. She remained drowsy from the effects of the meal and wine and wanted nothing more at that time than to be able to lie down and rest a while. But she forced herself to walk, step by step, until eventually it wore off.

At mid-afternoon, she was traveling directly toward the sun and again saw the spires of the castle looming on her left, no closer than they'd been earlier for all her walking. Riva sighed, wondering what kind of shelter she'd find that night. Would Leinad and Daniel find her again? If they did not, she'd miss them. She was in a worrying mood, for it occurred to her that should she complete the mission, she would be leaving the island, and leaving them behind. Her stomach twisted painfully at the thought of never seeing them again.

A little later, she turned at a slight bend in the road and saw another mist hovering ahead. She wasn't as worried about it this time as she'd been on previous occasions, but she wondered what it would portend.

Oddly, though, it didn't seem to portend anything. She waited for the sounds of voices, talking, and laughter that she'd experienced in the mists before, but it didn't happen. No one else lurked in the mist, and no voices called to her. Nothing at all out of the ordinary happened while she was passing through it.

When it finally lifted, after ten minutes or so, she was again aware of the day drawing to a close. She had only a single spare blanket and no food at all. What would she do for the night?

A wide gap in the trees to her left offered a nice view of the castle's spires and more of the building than she'd yet been able to see. With the sun gleaming off its sides, the walls of several towers and palisades had a silvery shimmer, while the light reflected off the roofs in sprays of gold.

Because she was looking up instead of at the road, she jumped nearly a foot in the air when a voice spoke to her.

"Greetings again, Princess," Varek said to her. He stood on the road, watching her with a sweet, sensual smile.

"Lord Varek," she said. "You said we'd meet again, but I guessed not 'twould be so soon."

"Aye, Princess. I could wait no longer. I know what you seek, and I would offer you help. Particularly, I would offer you a quicker way to the castle where you can claim the platter." He smiled again and bowed a little, nodding toward a break in the trees. "If you would follow me through here, I can show you a much faster way."

Riva watched him and debated. "Know you Leinad and Daniel? They've offered good advice and helped me. They told me I must stay on this road to make my way to the castle."

He laughed lightly. "I know them. They're good men, but rather careful and unadventurous."

"Yet they made a great sacrifice to gain me another chance after I failed a test."

Varek shook his head. "Do you not know you would have been given another chance anyway? Nay, I thought not. Come, you are a lady like myself. Direct, ambitious, and straightforward. Why do you continue to tread such a meandering and risky route? I can take you directly to the castle. I can show you how to find the platter and take it."

"And can you then show me the way from the castle and off the island again?"

His smile faded a bit. "Of course." A faint hesitation suggested to her that he was lying, or at least not telling the entire truth.

"And what recompense would you ask in return for this boon?"

"No more than anything you were willing to give," he said. "Come, you can be at the castle by sundown, if you would follow me."

Riva drew a breath. Again, she was tempted. She was tired, aching, and worried. She wanted this ordeal to be over. But would she be defeating herself if she accepted this offer and took the quicker way?

"I thank you for the offer, my lord," she said, "but I believe 'twould serve me better to continue on as I've been directed."

Varek sighed. "If you're sure that is your wish, Princess, I won't keep you."

Riva nodded sadly and walked on, not looking back. She couldn't help regretting that quick way to the castle. Her feet hurt, her bottom ached, and her head pounded.

With her spirits flagging and her body complaining, her progress slowed. The day waned and still she saw nothing that might serve as shelter. She began to search for a clear, grassy spot, where she might at least settle down on soft ground off the road. Even that eluded her.

Chapter Thirteen

The road twisted through a series of snake-like curves and up ahead she again saw a man waiting on the road. At first she couldn't distinguish the face or form, though his size suggested it couldn't be Varek. As she drew closer, she recognized Leinad.

Relief and joy spread through her. If she'd had the energy, she'd have run to greet him, but her exhausted body refused to hurry. He waited patiently for her to approach.

The twisted mouth split into its odd smile, while his golden brown eyes glowed. She threw herself into his arms and held on tight, almost overwhelmed by the pleasure of seeing him. He wrapped her up in his embrace.

"I'm overjoyed to see you here," he told her. "I know you've not had an easy day."

"'Twas a long one and hard."

"And you're now tired, hungry, and sore. Come with me and we'll fix those things as we may."

The exhaustion hadn't left her, but the promise of shelter and food gave her enough of a lift to carry her through a few more paces.

Leinad led her to the mouth of a cave. "Go on in." He stopped near the entrance. "Daniel's waiting. I'll see your horse settled for the night and then join you."

The tunnel she entered was high enough and wide enough to let her walk without stooping. After a short way, however, it grew quite dark, and she had to keep a hand on the wall, feeling her way forward carefully. On rounding a bend in the passage, a faint light glowing ahead beckoned her forward and illuminated the passage.

She negotiated a narrow arch and emerged into a much larger chamber, brightly lit by torches in brackets on the walls. On one side of the area stood a table, flanked by three chairs and set with three trenchers. A simple but broad bed, spread with plain linens, occupied the other side.

Daniel was removing items from a chest near the table. He stood and turned as she entered. A beautiful smile spread across his handsome face as he recognized her, and he came over to wrap her in a hug that surprised her with its intensity, since he was usually so reserved and undemonstrative.

"Welcome, Princess. I'm very glad to see you again." He backed up a step and looked her up and down. "You're tired and hungry. You can wash the dust off over there." He pointed to a sideboard that bore a basin and ewer. "As soon as Leinad comes in, we'll eat."

Leinad returned before she'd finished splashing the refreshing water over her face and hands. While they ate, she recounted her adventures of the day. Both men seemed pleased by her successes with the anthills and dogs, less so by her interaction with Varek.

"Was he correct that there was a quicker way to the castle I might take?" she asked them.

Daniel and Leinad looked at each other, and Leinad drew a deep breath. "Aye," he answered. "There are quicker ways."

"And would it have been a failure to take it?"

"Taking it would not have been a failure in itself. But it would have led to failure."

"I understand this not."

"And we may not explain any further." Leinad watched her with an almost pleading intensity. "We can only beg that you keep following this road. It *will* take you to your destination."

She nodded. When they finished the meal, the two men invited her to accompany them to another chamber, but they wouldn't tell her what she'd find there.

Blazing torches set in brackets in the rock wall lit the narrow passage they followed for some distance until it eventually opened up to a smaller, round chamber. Riva looked around the cave and felt her mouth drop open with the splendor of it.

The walls were lined with enormous, long, waving curtains of rock that fell from the ceiling to the floor of the chamber. Near the center of the space, narrow, jagged stone icicles hung from the ceiling. Water dripped off them and onto up-thrusting pyramids of stone below, running down them and collecting in a pool at the very center of the room. Torches were set into floor brackets. Their glow threw odd shadows on the stone walls and picked out rainbows of color on their damp surfaces.

"Magnificent," Riva whispered reverently as she scanned the amazing rock formation. Her words echoed around the room, again and again, then set up a pleasant, almost musical ringing from the rock itself. She'd never seen or heard anything like it.

Leinad and Daniel watched her awestruck astonishment with delight. "'Tis wonderful," Leinad agreed. His words set off another cascade of sound that flew around the cave. "And there is more. Come." He held out a hand and led her to the pool in the center. "Sit and put your feet in the water."

She sat down. She expected the water to be cold and hesitated to dip her toes into it. It was startlingly warm.

"'Tis fed from a warm spring below as well as from the drip above," Daniel explained. "It has a bent for healing small sores and relieving aching muscles also. Undress and slide in. You'll be able to stand in it."

He'd already shucked off his tunic and was releasing the lacing of his shirt. Riva watched both men undress, as much for the pleasure of studying their bodies as for waiting to see how they would react to the pool. Once both had slipped into it, and stood with the water lapping around them just above their waists, she removed her clothes and joined them.

The water had a strong aroma, akin to that of the sulfur matches they occasionally got from peddlers at home, and it felt different as well, somewhat heavier and grittier. When it touched the still-sore welts on her derriere, it stung a little. But the feel of it was so refreshing otherwise, so calming and soothing, yet invigorating at the same time, that the pain bothered her not at all.

The pool was large enough to accommodate the three of them easily without crowding but shallow enough that the water only came up to her breasts when she stood in it. They bounced up and down in the water, splashing gently and almost floating in it for a while. Daniel had brought soap and cloths. They soaped each other down. Actually, Riva spread soap on both men. She started with Daniel, spreading the lather over his lovely chest and shoulders, down his back to his buttocks and up to his hair, while Leinad watched and jibed about the poor, pale, bald creature she tended. Daniel's cock stood at hard, jutting attention before she finished, but when she reached for it, he stopped her. "Nay, lady. Not now."

"When then? 'Tis not fair that you tend to my need constantly, yet I may not do likewise for you."

"'Tis fair in ways you cannot yet understand," he answered. "I beg you, make this no harder for us than it already is."

She acceded to his plea and rinsed the suds from his body.

She washed Leinad next, working more of the soap lather into his fur, from his waist up along his chest to his head, then down his shoulders and back. When his wounds had been healed after the punishment, they'd apparently restored the fur that had been shaved off as well. Leinad sighed in obvious bliss as she massaged the suds in and rinsed them off. Daniel, watching, returned the digs about creatures with fur concealing their most interesting features. It didn't though, in her opinion. Leinad's cock, too, stood at turgid attention well before she finished.

Then they took a turn washing her. They soaped and rinsed her, pouring handfuls of water over her that trickled down her shoulders and breasts. They washed her hair and Leinad used his claws to finger comb it out of her face.

At their request, she stood on a rock near the side of the pool, which lifted her halfway out of the water, and faced away from them. She felt fingers trace the lines of the welts on her derriere. When a tongue followed, licking gently along the marks, she nearly jumped in startlement. It sent flashes of pure pleasure, like small streaks of lightning, flashing all through her. Her quim began to swell and get moist.

Leinad levered himself up out of the pool and sat on the edge with his furry feet and legs hanging into it. Daniel picked her up, turned her, and sat her in Leinad's lap, also facing toward the pool, with her feet dangling into the water. Furry arms wrapped around to hold her securely, but the paws each covered a breast and his claws gently explored her nipples. She gasped and moaned as more hot streaks of tingling pleasure shot through her.

Daniel moved closer to them. He lifted each of Riva's legs, parted them, and rested one on each of his shoulders. He reached forward and laid careful fingers on the petals of flesh at her slit, now opened to his view and touch. She was torn between closing her eyes to concentrate on the astonishing feelings they roused in her and opening them to watch the longing and delight mingle on Daniel's handsome face.

She squealed aloud when his fingers found her pearl and began to stroke it. Her body tightened, the pressure inside growing, a wave rising and rising, threatening to engulf her but not quite breaking.

Daniel dipped his head. The stroke of his tongue across her clit made her shriek with sheer, raw pleasure, almost too hot, too heavy to bear. He wrapped a hand around each of her legs to keep them in place as she began to writhe uncontrollably.

Leinad's claws pinched her nipples just hard enough to create a pleasure/pain mix that added to her ecstatic tension. He bent over to kiss her hair and forehead.

Daniel's fingers moved down, exploring the entrances to her body, while he sucked on her bud. His finger found the entrance to her womb and pushed gently inside. He lashed her clit lightly with his tongue.

Riva sobbed and moaned as the wave built and built. The sounds echoed oddly around the room, rising almost to a chorus, joyously counterpointing her growing tension.

It broke suddenly, the tide of pleasure rushing over her and engulfing her until she feared she'd drown in it. Her body spasmed repeatedly, each time sending a thrilling blast of pure pleasure through her. Gradually she relaxed into the warmth of the embrace of the two men. Her breathing quieted and the shaking calmed. She sank into exquisite peace.

After a while, Daniel shifted, took her legs from his shoulders and lifted her off Leinad's lap. They all wrapped up in towels, made their way back down the passage to the main chamber where they'd eaten, and piled into the bed. She reveled in the feel of them on either side of her for a moment before she sank into sleep.

Riva dreamed her fantasy lover again—the same dream, with a few small differences. He wore the mask and she could see only the golden brown eyes and the outline of his body in the dim light. Again she tried to escape, he caught her, carried her back to the room, rolled her over his knees and spanked her, then made love to her in a most exquisite and tender way.

There was no hint of fur when he caressed her, stroking, rubbing, licking, and nipping until she was in a frenzy of need. When she brushed the hair on his head with her hand, the length and texture of it felt much like Daniel's. The body that lay over hers when he moved to enter her felt like Daniel's as well.

He positioned himself with his cock brushing at the entrance to her womb, then he plunged deep. She cried out the first time, in surprise and at the depth of the feeling it aroused. With only short pauses, he pumped in and out. His balls slapped against her ass each time he buried himself, sending lightning bolt flashes of pleasure through her.

He stopped twice to kiss her, long, deep explorations of her mouth that had her writhing with need and desperate to bring him even more profoundly into her being. It felt as though he touched her soul as he pushed himself into her.

He filled her, completing her with their joining. He was so big, she felt stretched to accommodate him, but it was a supremely satisfying expansion.

Then he was pumping faster, harder, and the vibrations were rushing all over her body. She felt it in him, as well, the tightening of need, winding him into unbearable tension so that his body shook with it. He plunged into her in a frenzy of pressure, a fury of need that raged nearly out of control. After a few more hard pushes, he pulled out and she felt him go rigid. He rammed his cock home again. Hot seed spurted into her as her own need exploded into ecstasy with him, spasming in time with his shaking. They shouted simultaneously, in the wonder of a completion that took them to the far reaches of what a human being could bear.

The dream faded out while she still pulsed with the delight of it and stared into his golden brown eyes, meeting the expression of tenderness there.

She woke alone in the bed, but she rolled over and saw Daniel laying plates of food on the table.

Her dread grew as they ate. To divert her attention from what waited after the meal, she asked them about the cave.

"'Tis a part of the island," Leinad told her. "The island holds many wonders. Perhaps D'Jillan knows all of them, but no one speaks of it. We learn only what is needful for us to know."

It didn't tell her very much, but shed some light on how the island operated. "Who is D'Jillan?" she asked.

"The island's keeper. You met her the night of our penance," Leinad answered. "She can take many seemings, but most commonly she appears as a stately older woman. More than that I cannot say." He glanced at her plate. "Finish up now, Princess. There's naught to gain in delay, and perhaps something to lose."

She blushed at his realization of her attempt to stall. Her stomach tightened, and she could eat no more. She dropped her fork. "I'm finished."

Chapter Fourteen

They all stood. Daniel went to the trunk near the side of the room, and pulled from it a flat piece of wood about an inch wide and two feet long. Leinad took her in his arms and held her against him. "You have still some soreness from yesterday, so 'twill not be so severe today. Hold on to me."

Riva put her arms around him and locked her hands together behind his back. The length of wood didn't have the heft to bite deeply, though it roused a light sting where it slapped against her skin. The punishment was, as he'd promised, not so harsh as previous ones, though by the time Daniel had struck her a couple of dozen times, the flesh of her entire derriere burned. She panted and wiggled a bit in Leinad's hold during the last few strokes, but she didn't scream or cry this time.

When it was done, she clung to Leinad while she recovered and caught her breath. In truth, she enjoyed the feeling of being wrapped in his arms and didn't want to break the embrace. He nudged her gently and she stepped back away from him. She met his eyes for a moment, then turned to stare at Daniel. Both of them watched her with wistful, worried frowns.

"'Twas not so harsh today," Daniel said. "You'll move easier, and you might, perhaps, find the need to do so."

She didn't know what that meant but suspected they would not explain, so instead of asking about it, she drew a deep breath. "This is not easy for me to say," she told them. "I have not liked your punishments, yet I know they were light compared to what you both suffered. I know also that they have done me good, and so I thank you for it. I thank you for all you have done for me." Without breaking free of Leinad's hold, she leaned over and kissed Daniel on the cheek.

"We've already told you it benefits us as well, and therefore we're not so deserving of your thanks as you might believe," the latter answered.

"I understand that as well. Yet do I think you've done some hard things that have benefited me."

Daniel's frown lightened before Leinad's did, but both of them looked happier as they dressed and gathered their things together. Their expressions grew sadder again as she said her goodbyes to them and set out once more on the road. Her own heart twisted as she left them behind. She could only look forward to seeing them again that evening and wish she had their company on the journey itself.

The road continued its westerly course, and little of any interest occurred during the morning. Once or twice she saw the spires of the castle and began to speculate on what she would find once she got there. If she did get there. Leinad and Daniel had more or less promised her she would, if she remained on the road and passed the tests it threw at her.

Would she find crowds of people waiting for her at the castle? How would they greet her, especially when it became clear she wanted to take the platter? Would her tests be done when she got there, or would there be more?

Just before midday she encountered another mist and wondered what it would bring.

Almost immediately, she heard the sourceless voices and music that she'd noted before in connection with the fog. Laughter drifted around her and someone called to her with Leinad's voice. Again, though, it was neither forceful nor imploring, more just a suggestion of a request.

After a few minutes, she heard a different noise, one that sounded more like an animal than a person. The low, whining growl suggested a creature in pain. It grated on her nerves. She couldn't see far ahead in the mist, so she was almost upon it before she noted the figure just off the road on the side.

She had to get even closer before she could discern the form of a large, furry creature. It lay on its belly, head raised and swinging from side to side, but it didn't move otherwise. Riva halted the horse and stopped to study it. The animal wasn't on the road, but from its position, it could easily leap on someone passing there.

She took a few tentative steps forward. The creature's head swung around to stare at her, but it made no effort to intercept her. It was an enormous animal, with a long, round body and round, fur-covered head. Its long muzzle opened to show a frightening row of large, razor-sharp teeth. It snarled at her and shook itself.

It couldn't move because one of its legs was caught in a wicked-looking knot of barbed wire that also wound around several nearby trees. Iron thorns dug into the unfortunate beast's flesh. Blood stained and matted the fur into lumps near where the metal pierced it. Riva felt sorry for it but was also elated to realize she was safe from the creature's attack.

It dropped its head back onto its paws and gave another long, grating whine. The noise raked at her nerves and tightened her stomach. Almost, she wanted to help it, to at least turn it loose from the clutches of the loops of wire. A foolish notion, surely. The creature would rip her to shreds if she got close enough to try.

As she led the horse past on the road, the trapped beast moaned more loudly and whined in a way that sounded pleading. She tried not to look its way but couldn't help herself. Its eyes rested on her, its gaze a wordless plea that reinforced the pitiful moaning.

It would be terribly foolish to think she could do anything for it. Or would it? Perhaps there was a way to release it without getting too close. Riva led the horse past and some ways down the road. The mist still enclosed them, so the trapped animal disappeared from view quickly. Its grating moans continued to carry to her.

She tied the horse's reins to a tree at the side of the road and went back to take a look at the wire. When she came back in sight, the creature—it looked more like a bear than anything else—raised its head and bared its teeth at her.

Taking care to stay out of reach, she followed the length of barbed wire to where it was hooked into the low branches of a tree and caught in a shrub. Watching where she put her hands, she began to unwind the wire from the twigs trapping it. A couple of times the spikes scraped her hands when the animal pulled on the wire in its struggles to get loose. She wished she could use a spell to avoid having to handle the spiked wire itself, but with her limited ability to manipulate objects, it would take far too long.

Studying how the wire wrapped the creature's leg, she realized that if she could get around it a couple of times, and induce it to raise the leg, she might be able to free it without getting too close.

It was still only a possibility and not a very good one at that, plus it would take time, perhaps more than was wise, but she couldn't in good conscience leave the creature trapped without making some attempt to free it.

A stretch of open space behind the animal gave her room to maneuver. She pulled the wire in a wide arc around the creature. A couple of gentle tugs and a light "convince" spell finally induced him to lift the leg. Riva guided the wire carefully to slide it under his foot. Then she had to pray the bear-like animal knew enough or could sense enough of what she attempted to keep relatively still. If it struggled, it would likely wind itself back up in the wire. She couldn't do a strong enough spell to hold the creature in place for any length of time.

But it did remain quiet, watching her avidly. Riva tugged the wire back around in another circle. It took what seemed like a long time of nudging the wire, disentangling it when it caught on other branches, and pulling it away before she finally had it in position. One more twist and then another lift of the leg and the animal would be free.

Her heart rose into her throat when she realized that once the creature was loose it could easily turn and attack her. Maddened by the pain in its leg, and probably hungry as well, it might do just that.

She had neither sword to defend herself nor food to throw to distract it. If she took the time to go back to the horse, the creature would likely get itself tangled again. She either freed it now or left it to its fate.

Riva stood there, debating for a moment, but compassion won out. She wiggled the wire, sending another "convince" spell at the same time. The creature lifted its foot and then was loose. Riva froze, paralyzed by terror. The beast eyed her for a moment and she met its gaze. There was nothing else she could do. She couldn't move, couldn't run, couldn't yell for help or look for a place to hide.

Long moments passed as the animal watched her, but then it turned and shambled off on all fours into the underbrush. It limped a bit on the wounded leg, but moved fast enough to tell her the injury wasn't serious.

Relief made her legs rubbery. Cold sweat dripped down her face and sides. Several more long moments passed before she finally forced her wobbly legs to move.

She leaned against the horse for a moment after she freed the reins before they set out again.

Though she expected to walk out of the mist fairly soon after that, it didn't happen. The fog persisted for some time. The noises continued as well, and the sounds of people murmuring and laughing began to grow irritating. Worse yet, a voice kept calling her name repeatedly. It never grew louder or more insistent, but neither did it quit, and the sound began to work on her nerves.

As she continued, she found herself growing drowsy. Though she couldn't see the sun, she guessed it was a little past midday by then. She nibbled on some of the food Daniel had packed for her, eating while she walked. It didn't give her any burst of energy. In fact, it seemed to feed her growing lethargy. Her legs became leaden and each step was an effort. Finally she could fight it no longer, and when she found a nice stretch of grass on the side of the road, she spread a blanket, secured her horse, and lay down for a rest.

Riva was not sure if what she saw then was a dream or a vision. Either way it disturbed her.

A young man on horseback rode the same road she'd been following. Shadows hid his face from her, but the body was lithe and slim, the form of a young man. He held himself proudly, sure of his ability to defeat anything sent against him.

The pack of dogs she'd passed the previous day lurked ahead of him. Seeing the animals, the young man dismounted and drew a long, heavy sword. He secured his horse and walked toward the assemblage of animals. They pressed forward, snarling and growling. The man raised his sword.

When the first dog leapt toward him, he swung the sword. The other animals joined the fray, teeth bared and claws ready. The sword flashed, its metal surface gleaming in the sunlight. The third or fourth time she saw it rise, gore ran thickly along its length. Following an ugly interval of yelling, snarling, growling, and canine squalls, a reduced pack of dogs finally turned on their heels and ran away.

Five or six of the dogs lay dead or wounded on the road. The young man took a moment to catch his breath, then wiped his sword on the grass, mounted his horse, and proceeded on his journey. As he turned to head back up the road, she caught a brief glimpse of a beautiful face with dark hair and golden brown eyes. Daniel.

When she woke, the mist had passed off. For a moment she panicked with the worry she'd slept far too long. But the sun still rode high in the sky, just beginning to move off in the direction she was proceeding on the road. After a deep, steadying breath, she shook off the remaining drowsiness and got to her feet.

She couldn't shake off the effects of the dream quite so easily. Had the man in her dream truly been Daniel? Was she seeing how he'd failed the island's test? Yet no Gatekeeper had appeared to tell him about it. Could that have happened after her vision had ended? If so, how long ago had it happened?

Towards mid-afternoon, she noted the road beginning to change direction, turning southward. Twice she saw again the top of the castle. From this side she could also see a large, square main building rising in stately splendor, topped with ramparts and a series of turrets. Dishearteningly, she didn't seem to be any closer to it.

She couldn't help but wonder what the night would bring. She hoped to see Leinad and Daniel again. Could she ask Daniel about the vision of him fighting the dogs? She wasn't quite sure that what she'd seen wasn't just a dream.

The next obstacle appeared with no warning late in the afternoon. In a place where branches from several large, old trees hung over the road, forming a sort of narrow tunnel, a sharp whizzing sound alerted her to something odd going on. Bare seconds later, several enormous birds flew out of the concealment of the leafy branches, diving at her. They had long, sharp beaks, all pointed straight in her direction.

Riva grabbed her sword from its sheath, but had to duck as the first bird soared toward her. It sailed right over her head, but several more were behind it. One sharp beak grazed her arm as she shifted to bring her sword around in front of her.

More birds poured out of the tree, and the first wave circled around for another pass at her. She'd never seen anything like these creatures, another wonder of the island. They were several feet long, with an even wider wingspan, and had lean, bony bodies to go with the long sharp beaks. She had no time to speculate on what they might be, however.

One after another, and sometimes in groups of two or three, they came at her. She waved the sword in front of her, using it to protect her face and chest. She made contact with a few of them, even beheaded one that dared to come straight at her in defiance of the sword. Sharp beaks sliced at her arms and sides, however, and no matter how many times she dodged, they continued to circle around and come back at her in near continuous waves.

Riva had no idea how to defeat them all. She'd killed one and disabled a couple of others by breaking wings or smashing beaks, but there were probably two dozen or more left. She was already bleeding in places and bruised in even more. The odds favored the birds. They attacked her horse, too, and she finally took pity on her mount and released it to run away. She barely had time to watch it disappear, running down the road. A couple of birds tried to chase it, but the horse outran them.

Without the horse, Riva felt desperately alone. She shouted and yelled as she swung at more of the attacking birds, hoping someone would hear and come to her assistance.

Bones in one of the birds' wings snapped under a swipe from her sword, but another one used the distraction to attack her uncovered side. Just in time, Riva dodged the other way and avoided a puncture from that wicked beak. She breathed hard and her arms burned from the effort of swinging her weapon. She beheaded another one, but couldn't avoid the one that came at her low, tearing the fabric of her leggings and scratching the flesh below.

She screamed and attacked more fiercely, driven by the sting of the cuts they inflicted.

When she'd decided that no help would be forthcoming, and that she was likely fighting for her life and doomed to lose, help did arrive. It wasn't exactly the help she was expecting.

As the pack of dogs ran up behind her, snarling and growling, she felt certain for a few minutes that she was doomed even more surely than before. It wasn't until they began to leap toward the birds, teeth snapping and claws waving, that she realized they were allies. She was too busy defending against another mass attack from the birds to see exactly when the bear-like creature she'd rescued that morning arrived also. But it was even more effective than the dogs were. It swung massive arms, knocking aside the pointed beaks and tossing the birds hard against the trees and into the ground. A couple of the dogs got hold of wingtips or tail feathers and battered the captured birds up and down until they smashed against the ground.

Riva sliced a wing off one bird and a leg off another before the flock apparently recognized they were outnumbered. A series of squawks broke out among them, growing to almost deafening intensity, and then the entire group veered off, swung around, and flew back into the concealment of the trees.

Riva bent over, struggling to catch her breath. The dogs milled for a moment, looking for more prey, while the beast stood watching for the birds to return. She wondered if they would attack her now that their other foes had disappeared.

It didn't happen. The pack of dogs finally gave up and turned as a group to run back down the road, though a few picked up dead birds in their mouths to take with them. The beast also left, disappearing into the shrubbery. She hadn't even thanked them, though the only way she could think that she might have done so would be to offer them food. She would have done it if they'd waited a bit longer. Or she would have liked to. Since her food had gone along with her horse, she realized she had nothing to offer.

The sun rode low on the horizon by then. Riva struggled to collect her wits and get moving again. She hoped it would be obvious where she was supposed to spend the night, and that it wouldn't be much farther.

She ached from bruises where the birds had bumped her. Cuts on her arms and one along her side stung ferociously. If there were any poison in those wounds, she needed help quickly.

She began to worry about that as a serious possibility when her vision blurred and dizziness washed over her in waves. It took an enormous exertion to force herself to keep moving. Each step was an effort, every movement a victory of will over the desire to lie down and sleep.

It seemed like a long time before she came to anything. While she walked, the sun sank lower and the light faded. More than once she lost track of where she was and what she was doing. When she forgot all else, however, she remembered that she needed to keep moving along the road.

Twilight had spread across the land when she finally saw something ahead in the distance that made her rub her eyes to be sure it wasn't an illusion. It was such a welcome sight, she hardly believed it real. She squinted and hoped. Her horse stood in the center of the road, his reins clutched in Daniel's hand.

Though her legs wobbled and threatened to give way, and darkness spread across the land, obscuring her vision, the sight of Daniel kept her moving. He came to meet her, leading the horse.

Riva tried to say something to him, to tell him how glad she was to see him, but she'd reached the limits of her endurance. She faded out completely.

Chapter Fifteen

She dreamed again. At first they were just wild bits of vision, people telling her things she couldn't understand, animals flying at her, places she'd never seen before, and occasionally a deep shadow enveloping her in a frightening nothingness. Beasts chased her, attacked her, fell on her, and tore at her. Then she was floating, peacefully, in a calm sea of water, rocked by gentle waves.

Once she ran down an apparently endless corridor, approaching a deep red light—or maybe pursued by it. Doors opened along the corridor and weird, shadowy figures yelled orders at her. She shouted back at them. Some of them invited her to enter the rooms they guarded, but she declined each time.

She ran through fire at one point, dodging flames all around, searching for a cooler spot. Sweat poured off her body as the blaze licked at her. Her hair caught fire and she had to squeeze the flames out of it. It scorched her fingers.

Then she was in a more peaceful place, surrounded by broad swaths of green grass. A herd of placid cows grazed nearby and songbirds hovered in trees overhead. The sun beat down, warm and comforting. A stream babbled not far off to her left.

The scene changed to a richly appointed bedroom, where she stood between two men. Oddly, both were her dream lover, tall, dark figures, masked and cloaked, their faces just barely visible. Only the golden brown eyes of each showed clearly. One of the two might have had fur on his face and arms, but she couldn't see well enough to be certain.

They both tried to embrace her and interfered with each other in the attempt. They looked at each other and then at her. "You'll have to choose between us," the one told her. The other added, "You cannot have us both. Make your decision wisely. You'll have only one chance."

"How can I choose?" she asked, in the dream. "I love you both. I want you both."

"It cannot be," the one told her.

"We cannot exist together," the other said. "You must choose which of us you'll have."

Anger and dismay mixed to upset her. How could they demand this from her? "I know not how!"

"Make your choice," the first one insisted.

"Not yet. I'll need to think on it in order to choose properly."

"Think then," the second one said. "Yet take not too much time in the deciding lest the choice be made for you."

"I just don't know how. I cannot choose." She sobbed until it felt as though her heart broke. But she faded out again before she made any decision.

* * * * *

She had no idea how much later it was when she woke. She lay on a soft, comfortable bed in a large room with surprisingly luxurious appointments. She looked around, studying the velvet bed curtains, pulled to the corners, dark wood chests, wardrobe against the walls, a stand with a basin and ewer of water, and long, rich drapes covering two windows. Sunlight crept through the gaps in the drapery. No one else was in the room.

Bandages covered her arms. A strong smell of herbs infused the cloths wrapping her. When she tried to move, she found it easier than she anticipated. She'd expected the various bruises to ache, but in fact, she realized while pushing herself up to a sitting position, she felt surprisingly well.

A door on the far side of the room squeaked and opened to admit Leinad. The frown on his ugly face broke into a wide grin when he saw her. He crossed the room to stand over her. "How do you now, Princess? We were worried for you. It appeared the poison might be too deeply run into your system."

"I'm well. Quite well. You used strong medicine, I think, and it has done its task. But what were those creatures that attacked me?"

"Kelzars. Nasty birds. Their beaks bear a mild poison, though it usually does no more than make one weak for a while. You got a rather large dose of it, however, and it took the night to work it out of you. You had us worried for a time, but now you should do well enough. Are you hungry?"

Riva consulted her stomach and found it more than eager for food. "Aye."

Assisted by Leinad, she dressed and made her way out of the room. They walked down a long hall, paneled in rich, dark wood and hung with numerous tapestries, to a room that was smaller but no less richly furnished.

"Where are we?" she asked.

"The home of a friend," Leinad answered. "She allowed us to avail ourselves of its facilities for the night."

Daniel entered through a different door, carrying a tray of food. He smiled at her. "You look more healthy now than when last I saw you. It gladdens me. Will you take some food?"

"Aye, and I thank you."

They ate well. The ordeal of the previous day had left her with an enormous appetite, which she indulged heartily.

As the meal went on, though, she noted that Leinad's and Daniel's moods seemed to darken. The relief of seeing her awake and healthy faded into some other worry or concern. Trepidation grew inside her as well, when she considered that it was morning and she was due for another session of their discipline.

When they were done with the meal, they asked her to come with them back to the bedroom. All three of them were quiet as they retraced the way down the hall to the room.

She was surprised when they didn't immediately tell her to prepare for punishment. Instead they asked her to have a seat on the side of the bed.

Leinad paced across the room a couple of times before he stopped, faced her, and heaved a deep breath. "I have some things to tell you, and most of them are not pleasant or easy. I wish it could be otherwise, and I would not have to tell you what I am about to. But wiser minds than mine rule the affairs of the island, and they say this is how it must be." He walked back and forth a few more times as though bracing himself.

Riva's stomach clenched and her heart tightened in dread. If he was this unhappy about what he had to say, it would definitely not be something she wanted to hear.

How much worse could the tests the island threw at her get? Or had she failed yesterday with the birds? Would he tell her she must leave and never come back, or face the headman's axe? Her stomach twisted and clenched painfully. Sorrow assailed her when she considered she might never see Leinad or Daniel again. She'd come to prize their love and friendship that much.

Leinad interrupted her unhappy musings when he finally brought himself to speak again. "This is the last time you'll see us until you get to the castle. If all goes well 'twill take you only two more days, but we'll not be meeting you this evening. Should you make it past any obstacles this day you'll come to a small cabin towards evening. You may take your rest there and eat whatever you find in the place."

He sighed audibly. "Before we send you on your way, there are other things I must tell you. Go boldly but carefully. Be not afraid. You don't go entirely alone, though you may see no one accompanying you. You've learned much. Remember all. Take care for all. Harm no one and nothing save that it attempts to harm you first."

Leinad looked over at Daniel. The latter nodded encouragement. Riva worried about what he seemed so reluctant to say, since it appeared she hadn't yet failed and been ejected from the island.

"When you get to the castle," Leinad added, "you'll find a few more challenges. One will be to find your way to the room where the platter resides. When you get there you'll see us again. And there you will be asked to do something you will find…difficult. Nay, more than that. You'll not believe anything so…outrageous could be asked of you, and you'll want to refuse. You will wonder that anyone could ask you to do such a deed. And you will also face a terrible decision that you must make."

He drew another deep breath, came to her, knelt down in front of her, and took her hands in his furry paws. "I beg you to listen to me now and trust what I tell you. You must do what is asked. No matter how much it horrifies or pains or appalls you. Trust that all will come out well, though you may not see how that can possibly be so. 'Twill be difficult for you, without doubt, the hardest thing you've ever been asked to do. And 'twill seem wrong to you as well. But it must be done, and it must be done by you. Choose as wisely as you may, and do what is needful."

He wore a serious frown. Almost he appeared to be in pain.

What would be required must be terrible indeed, but did he not have faith in her to complete the quest, no matter how hard the final test might be? "I do not understand," Riva admitted.

"You cannot as of now," Leinad said. "But 'twill become clear, and I hope you'll remember my words then."

"I will."

"'Tis all I can ask. And now, a reminder for you. The last you'll receive from us." He drew her to her feet and helped her undress.

He pulled her into his arms and held her firmly. She didn't see what implement Daniel had, but the whizzing sound it made in delivering the first stroke sounded like the leather strap he'd used the very first time. It cracked against her flesh like leather, as well, and the pain was a ribbon of fire across her derriere. She hissed through her teeth as she fought against making any sound.

More than a dozen strokes later, she squirmed in Leinad's hold and dug her fingers into his back. Her bottom was on fire, the entire surface fiery hot and stinging more than she'd thought she could bear. But each blow roused the deeper fire that made her quim swell and moisture seep down her legs. Some of her moans came from pain, others from a need deeper than either pain or pleasure.

"Courage, my dear," Leinad implored, patting her back to try to soothe her. But nothing could keep her calm when one last splat of the leather sent waves of agony washing up and down through her. She squealed and tried to kick out, sobbed, moaned, writhed, and rubbed herself frantically against his leg

When it was over, Leinad picked her up and carried her to the bed. As before they worked a soothing salve in her flesh, and as before the touch of their fingers on that super-sensitive skin caused a heavy throbbing in her clit. The pain faded but the tingling left behind worked its way deep into her loins. The next time she groaned, it wasn't from pain, but from longing.

When they moved her legs apart, she sighed. Fingers stroked up and down her thighs. Heat surged through her, making her tighten.

Together they rolled her over onto her back. She moaned when her sore bottom touched the sheets, but it transmuted again into excitement and pleasurable tension. Leinad positioned himself between her legs and began stroking her, his furry fingers providing an entirely new and delightful sensation on her flesh. Daniel moved over her breasts, holding the tip of one between his fingers and dipping his head to suck on the other.

They stroked, petted, sucked, licked, and nipped her into a writhing, moaning frenzy of passionate need.

Neither appeared to be in a hurry, and in fact, they seemed determined to go slowly and savor every moment of the experience. Long before they were ready to let her come, she was thrashing and groaning, begging them to go faster and finish it. Her pleas didn't move them. They continued their slow, maddening stroking and working on her until Riva was driven nearly mad by the pressure of need.

They moved again so that she lay on her side, sandwiched between them, though their heads were both positioned at the level of her groin. Leinad, behind her, lifted her top leg and let it rest on his shoulder. He kissed the sore spaces on her bottom over and over, soothing the aches with his tongue, while his fingers traced down the crack that separated the cheeks until he got to her rear hole. He explored its edges and bounds for a few minutes before he pushed the tip of a finger inside.

It burned at first and she moaned, but he pushed steadily. The new fullness added another layer to her pleasure and need.

Daniel meanwhile, was working on her clit, stroking and massaging it until the pressure screamed through her, demanding release.

Twice they brought her right to the edge of exploding, then drew back before it happened. They waited a moment before starting to build her up again. The third time, though, they could no longer keep the wave of her release from exploding in a tide of spasms that rocked her for long minutes, bringing a pleasure too deep and high to hold onto for long. Her sighing moans were a song of delight, paced by the rhythm of her pulsing around the finger still impaling her.

Even when her release had crested and begun to wane, they continued to stroke her as though they could not get enough of feeling her. If they expected not to see her again for a while then perhaps that explained why they were so reluctant to let her go now. She wasn't at all sure she wanted them to stop. But eventually her body could bear no more. She reached over first to Leinad and then to Daniel, touching their faces. They moved up so that they could press the lengths of their bodies against her on either side. It was the warmest, most secure and thoroughly satisfactory position she could ever remember being in.

She pressed a hand to each erect cock. "May I?" she asked. "A gift as we are to be parted for a time?"

Leinad and Daniel looked at each, then both shook their heads. "Nay, Princess," Daniel answered. "Much though we do wish it." He said the words so wistfully, she knew them for no less than the truth. "We may not now. If all goes well, there will be a time for this."

Both men rose and dressed, then helped her get up and prepare to depart.

She came down from the ecstasy of their lovemaking to the reality that when she left the building they occupied, she wouldn't see them again for a while. The next time they met, she'd face a harder test than any that had come before.

Riva kissed each of them and fought the urge to cling. If she passed whatever tests remained, she would see them again.

Chapter Sixteen

As she set out along the road again, she couldn't help but muse on Leinad's words and what they might portend. What kind of terrible thing could they ask of her? Something that involved desperate pain? Would she be required to surrender her life in return for the platter?

What else might it mean? But how would it benefit her family should she die? Would her father be granted the platter anyway? Perhaps, then, it would be worth whatever it might cost her.

Daniel had said there would be a time, though, when she could bring them fulfillment, if all went well. That surely suggested she wouldn't be required to die...or did it? She couldn't sort it out.

The road headed south for most of the morning, but toward midday, she noticed it begin to bend to the east. She waited for a mist or some obstacle to appear on the road, but it didn't occur until an hour or so later. When the foggy patch appeared ahead, Riva marched toward it, wondering what sort of challenge it would bring.

The voices called to her, the invisible people spoke and laughed together. She didn't see anything or meet anyone for a time. The fog lifted and she went on some distance before anything interest occurred.

At first glance, there was nothing unusual about the scene that unrolled before her when she went round a bend in the road. A group of modest houses formed a small village. At a stream running nearby, women took a break from washing the clothes that were strewn all over the grass, drying in the sun. They sat on several sheets or blankets with food spread out before them. The group hailed her as she went past.

"Lady," they called. "Would you break your journey and take a meal with us? We have plenty."

Since they offered the food, Riva thought it would be churlish to refuse. And since they apparently lived so close to the castle, they might give her some helpful information.

"I thank you." She led the horse onto the grass, tacked down the reins and joined the group. "I'm Riva."

Two of the women slid over to make room on one of the blankets for her. They passed her slices of bread and fruit and asked about her journey.

"Are you going to the castle?" one of the women asked, after they'd each identified themselves.

"Aye," Riva answered. "I'm told this road will take me there, though in truth, 'tis not the most direct way."

"Nay, 'tis not that, Lady Riva," they agreed. "Though it will get you there."

"Have you been in the castle yourselves?"

Several of them nodded. "Aye, lady. We serve there when there's need."

"Who is the lord of the castle?"

They gave her an odd look. "The Keeper, of course."

"Is not D'Jillan the Keeper? What is the Keeper's role? Is there no king or queen?"

That apparently perplexed them. "The Keeper is…The Keeper. We need no others."

She gave up trying that line of questioning. "Do they hold feasts in the castle or have carnivals?"

"On occasion there's a great feast," one woman answered.

"At times, but not so often," another added.

"What occasions call for a feast?"

They looked around at each other and shrugged. "When The Keeper says 'tis time for a feast," one answered, her tone making it clear the answer should have been perfectly obvious.

Riva decided to change course entirely. "Do you know a pair of men named Leinad and Daniel? Though I am not sure if Leinad is truly a man."

Several of the women frowned and muttered. "We know them," the woman who seemed to be the main spokesperson for them said. "As well as they can be known. They're not truly what they seem. Not at all. Be cautious in trusting them."

"They've given me much help."

"They had their own reasons for doing so. Be not so sure they acted solely to further your interests. Do not believe they have told you all the truth."

This was definitely not the kind of information Riva had been looking for. She needed to believe in Leinad and Daniel. They'd helped her and given her good advice. They'd sacrificed for her. If she couldn't trust them, she felt lost. She knew Leinad and Daniel better than she knew these women. But even Leinad had admitted that they were pursuing their own interests in aiding her.

When they'd finished eating, the women stood and began to collect the clothes they'd washed. Riva thanked them for sharing their food, freed the horse's reins, and set out again.

She saw the spires and keep of the castle rising still on her left, but she was no closer to it. The road curved around toward the east, which meant she'd made a near-complete circle around the castle. If she didn't find the entrance to it soon, she'd be back at the place where she'd come onto the island and started out on this road. If Daniel and Leinad had lied to her about the road taking her to the castle, she could be going around and around. Yet the women had agreed this way would take her to her destination.

Nonetheless, Riva began to wonder if she should leave the road and search for a path that would take her more directly to her destination. As the afternoon wore on, the temptation to seek out another, faster way grew on her. She'd gone so far and was becoming weary of the journey.

The mist caught her by surprise this time, descending suddenly and with no warning. She didn't see it coming at all. One minute she walked in bright sunlight, the next moment the fog had enveloped her.

It made her uneasy. She slowed the pace, wondering what might happen, and waited to hear the voices and calls that normally came with the mist. Silence surrounded her.

She kept walking through the fog, alert for what challenge might come. The only thing that occurred was that she became dizzy and somewhat groggy. She rubbed her eyes when they began to burn. Her vision clouded. It became so bad after a few minutes, she had to stop. Hoping that keeping her eyes closed for a bit would restore her sight, she found a clearing, lay down to rest, and let her lids slide down.

When she looked again, she couldn't tell if what she saw was real or a vision. The fog still surrounded her, letting her see only a few feet in any direction. Something dreamy about the way the mist swirled around her in whitish waves gave an unreal aspect to the scene. The trees didn't loom over her in the same way she'd thought they'd done just before she'd closed her eyes. A branch had hung down near the road to her left, but it was gone now.

Leaves that were green when she closed her eyes now appeared orange-gold as though the season had changed to fall in a blink. Not far from her, but partially obscured by the mist, stood two men. They faced each other, poised and tense. When each one raised a sword, the breath caught in her throat.

A sob tore from her as she recognized the two figures. Leinad and Daniel. They lunged at each other. Bright metal blades met and crossed with a loud clang. They drew back, circled each other, and pressed forward again. The noise rang and echoed in her ears. Time and again, their swords struck at each other, high, low, to the left of the figures and to the right. Blades pointed at the opponent's hearts and stabbed at their targets, only to be diverted by the opposing blade.

At one point, Leinad worked Daniel back until he slammed up against a tree and seemed destined to be run through. But at the last possible second, Daniel ducked, whirled around, and brought his sword back up. He mounted a furious offensive until Leinad had to give ground.

Daniel landed a stroke that sliced up Leinad's arm, making the blood run. Several more furious flurries of crossing swords, feints, and retreats ensued. One retreated, then pushed forward, then the other did so. Each dripped blood from several small cuts before it ended.

The two closed together, the blades sliding up alongside each other as their bodies pressed toward each other. Their swords caught between them as the two jammed together practically nose to nose. One of them gave a loud shout. The pair stood obscenely still for a moment, frozen in place, both faces twisted in strain or agony. Then one of them began to collapse to the ground.

The mist thickened, and she couldn't see which of them it was.

Chapter Seventeen

The fog grew so dense she couldn't see her own hand when she raised it in front of her face. It burned her eyes so fiercely, she had to blink tears away.

When she opened her eyes again, the scene had changed. The mist thinned and the trees were leaved in green once more. The branch hanging near the road partly blocked the way.

What she'd seen before must have been a vision or a dream. Riva walked up the road to the place where the men had fought and examined the ground. No bloodstains showed in the dirt. There should have been marks, scuffs, a broken branch where one of them had nearly tripped, but nothing provided any evidence that a fight had truly taken place there.

What did it mean? Why would Leinad and Daniel be fighting each other? Did one of them fall beneath the other's sword?

The island offered no answers.

Riva set out again. The mist dissolved before she'd gone far, leaving the afternoon sun to beat down on her. Nothing else happened for some time, and she walked on, watching the spires of the castle appear and disappear from view.

As the sun sank lower in the sky, she began to look for the cabin Leinad had said she'd find. Her feet hurt, legs ached, and sweat plastered her clothes to her body. The questions piling up in her mind added a form of spiritual weariness. She'd always been so sure of herself, so certain of what was right and wrong, so sure she knew when she could trust someone. The world felt upside down and topsy-turvy.

She kept trudging on, beginning to wonder if the entire trip was a fool's errand. Had she been deceived into believing she could succeed in this quest, or was she going about it entirely the wrong way, trusting the wrong people for advice and direction?

It was growing dark by the time she saw a small building looming in the distance. Riva hurried forward, eager for rest and food.

The cabin was small and rough, both inside and out, almost depressingly normal. The single main room held a narrow, hard bed, a table with two chairs and a cupboard. A pitcher of water rested on the table, along with a small loaf of bread and a couple of dried, salted fish. Since she'd been granted permission by Leinad to use the cabin and its facilities, Riva dropped her pack and poured a cup of water.

She settled the horse behind the cabin, then went back in and ate the food left for her. Despite their warning that she wouldn't see them again until she got to the castle, she kept waiting for Leinad and Daniel to show up. She'd grown so used to them appearing when she wasn't looking that she kept glancing over her shoulder, waiting for something to happen. It didn't, and she retired to the bed shortly after she finished her dinner.

Given all the doubts and uncertainties, she expected to have trouble falling asleep, but that didn't happen either.

Her dreams, though, kept the sleep from being restful. Some of them were unspecific and vague but distressing nonetheless. She found herself in a long, dark corridor again, wondering what was at the and knowing she didn't really want to get there to see. Even worse, at times she couldn't move at all. It felt as though her feet were glued to the floor or mired in mud.

Later, the dream vision grew clearer and even more distressing.

She saw the platter, sitting on a table, tipped on its side, much as it had been the first night she'd been on the island. But as she watched, two men, their faces and forms hidden by voluminous, hooded cloaks, approached and lifted the platter from its resting place. They began to carry it toward a nearby door.

She waited for someone to intervene, to try to stop them. Nothing happened. They got to the door and carried it through and outside. A trio of horses waited for them. They fastened the platter to one of the horses and then they each mounted one of the others.

As they rode down the road, the platter on its own mount between them, she finally got a view of their faces. Her heart had already recognized them, however. Leinad and Daniel.

Taking the platter away. She wanted to run after them, to berate them for their betrayal, to beg them to come back, to curse them for stealing what she sought.

Morning sunlight pouring in through the window woke her. More food had appeared on the table, so she ate quickly and set out again. If Leinad had told her the truth, today she should reach the castle. It had best be so. If she didn't arrive soon, she would likely find herself back where she started.

She couldn't help wondering about the dream that remained so vivid in her memory. Was it a true vision or something her imagination had conjured? If it were true, why should she trust anything Leinad or Daniel had said?

The road continued bending around toward the east and the spires of the castle loomed tantalizingly on her left. Was it just wishful thinking that suggested they appeared closer than they had previously?

Riva fought the depressing suspicion the entire trip was in vain, that she'd been fooled and betrayed. She'd begun to care about them, too.

She shook herself. It was a dream. She had no idea if it were true. She couldn't assume it was.

She was getting so weary. Her back, feet, legs, and sides ached from days of walking.

No mists appeared through the morning. The only thing that interrupted the journey before noon was a surprise meeting with Varek, who waited by the side of the road. He greeted her with a broad smile.

"Surely you're tired of this journey, Princess," he said. "You've been traveling for days, and yet you're little closer than you were when first we met."

"I am weary. But I was promised this road would take me to the castle. In fact, I was told I should arrive this very day if all went well."

Varek tipped his head to one side. "Aye, and so it will. But did they warn you about the tunnel and what it would bring? Did they tell you you'd have to find your way through the labyrinth inside should you enter by this way?"

"Nay, they said naught of those things. I believe there was a reason they did not."

"Perhaps so," Varek said. "Perhaps they wanted to ensure they would secure the platter for themselves. They came here on a quest for it, just as you have, you know."

"I know that. They said our fates were entwined, as was our success and failure."

"I can show you an easier way to the castle. A way that will take you there without your having to walk the tunnel or the labyrinth. 'Twill have you there within the hour."

She was tempted. Very tempted. She didn't like the sound of the "tunnel" or the "labyrinth". She just wanted to get the platter and get back to her family. But then, she wouldn't see Leinad and Daniel again. It seemed that no matter what happened, some heartache would result.

"I—" She stopped in the act of accepting his offer. No matter how much doubt she had about Leinad and Daniel's motives, she believed them when they said the way for her to win the platter lay in remaining on the road. When they met again, they could explain the dreams to her.

"I thank you, sir," she answered. "But I believe I must stay on the road."

"'Twill not be an easy way into the castle," Varek warned. "Why must you insist on doing this in such a difficult way when an easier one is available? You make it harder than it must be."

"Aye, it seems I do so. Yet, I was told there are no shortcuts. I must take the road the entire way if I'm to gain the platter. That is my challenge, and I must meet it."

He shook his head. "So be it then, Princess. Grace be with you on the way. You will need it."

Riva thanked him for his concern and the offer of help, and then proceeded on her way, struggling to keep herself upright and moving.

The day grew hotter than it had been since her arrival. Sweat soaked her clothes and stung her eyes when it dripped down her temples into them. Her shoulders sagged. Damp hair hung over her forehead and clung to her neck. Fiery pains shot up and down her legs each time she moved. Could she truly make it to the castle that day?

A little past noon, she met another person on the road and recognized one of the women who'd been washing clothes yesterday. The woman stopped and greeted her.

"Lady," she said. "You're going to the castle and still on this road?"

"Aye. I was told I must if I would gain the object of my quest here."

The woman nodded. "You must get to the castle, but there are easier ways than staying on this road. If you would, I can show you a way that will bring you to the castle within minutes. 'Tis just a short walk from here. Would you come?"

The temptation to accept was even stronger this time. Every limb and muscle burned. Fear of what would still be required of her further flayed her drooping spirit. Yet did she still believe the road was the proper way.

Leinad and Daniel had promised it was so. They'd proved trustworthy so far.

They wanted the platter themselves, and they'd set her on a road that wound around and around her destination, without, apparently ever reaching it.

They'd promised she would reach it, and had truly given her no reason to doubt their word. They'd warned her to stay on the road, that it offered her the best chance of success.

After a few more minutes of internal debate, Riva thanked the woman but declined the offer. She set out again, leaving the woman shaking her head in disbelief and confusion.

The day got hotter and hotter and she grew ever more weary. Her spirits flagged as exhaustion engulfed her. She began to regret the decision to continue on the road rather than take one of the more direct routes she'd been offered. Even the horse seemed discouraged and tended to lag if she didn't keep tugging at the reins. She ate the last of the food she'd brought and hoped she'd reach the castle before starvation set in.

Just beyond mid-afternoon, the road bent around to the north again. Within minutes, the spires of the castle loomed over her, directly ahead. The main keep, a lovely, white-washed box six stories high, soon came into view. Sunlight reflecting off its side bathed it in a silver glow. Watchtowers rose from a tall wall that surrounded it, along with several separate towers and outbuildings whose presence she deduced from the glimpses of roof she could see.

The road plunged on ahead, racing straight toward the imposing two-story, brick wall and the huge gap cut into it. An enormous, heavy iron portcullis barred entry into the main courtyard. A cube-shaped box for a lookout stood beside the gate atop the wall. She couldn't see if anyone occupied it. The road continued into the castle grounds. Beside the main gate, smaller doors on either side possibly provided an alternate method of entry.

Riva halted in front of the gate, waiting for someone to acknowledge her presence. Someone should have seen her from the guardhouse, but nothing happened. She shaded her eyes and looked up. With the slanting rays of the afternoon sun glowing into it, she couldn't tell whether anyone occupied the cubicle or not.

"Greetings!" she called as loudly as she could. "I'm a visitor, come in peace. I seek entrance."

If anyone heard her, they chose not to acknowledge it. Riva waited a few moments before repeating her greeting. Still no one answered. The iron bars of the portcullis remained stubbornly in place.

"I beg your attention," she added after a pause to allow response. "I request entry. I'm a lone lady, come in peace."

And still nothing moved, no one appeared, no one answered her pleas.

Gritting her teeth against the frustration, Riva moved forward. She tried the portcullis, to see if it could be pushed or moved, but wasn't surprised when it refused to budge. A glance through the bars showed no one moving in the courtyard or anywhere within her range of vision. She searched for a bell, gong, or some other way of notifying the guards of her presence. Nothing.

She wiped away the sweat dripping into her eyes and turned to the smaller doors on either side of the gate. The one on the right refused to move when she tried the latch, and she could neither push nor pull it. Riva leaned against it for a moment, fighting tears of combined exhaustion and frustration.

Struggling against threatening depression, she went to the other door. Because she really didn't expect it to open, she almost fell in when the door swung inward at the touch of her hand.

What she found on the other side was even more surprising than the ease with which the door opened.

Chapter Eighteen

Instead of coming out into the sunlit courtyard, as she expected, she faced a blank wall in front of her, no more than an arm's length from the entrance. A very dark hallway stretched off to the left. She peered that way, waiting for her eyes to adjust to the dimmer light, but even then she couldn't see very far down its length. It was wide enough and tall enough to accommodate the horse, but she wasn't sure it was a good idea to bring the animal.

In the end, though she still had doubts about the wisdom of it, she elected to bring her mount. If she left him, he might have to wait there for days without water or food. She just prayed the corridor wouldn't narrow too much to let him pass or end in some impossible corner.

She set off down the corridor, leaving the door open to admit a little bit of light. Once beyond that slice of daylight, it became very dark and she had to fire the single torch she had with her. She hoped the corridor wasn't too long, as the torch wouldn't last more than an hour or so. The way remained level, but widened out somewhat as she proceeded. Riva couldn't help but wonder where it was taking her.

The corridor twisted gently to the right. For a while, she had to keep a hand on the wall and watch her steps carefully. The horse wasn't happy about the conditions and balked a couple of times. It took considerable persuasion to keep him moving.

The torch didn't last even the hour she'd hoped, but when it flickered and died out, the darkness wasn't as complete as she'd anticipated.

A faint light glowed ahead. It helped illuminate the way, but it also showed that the corridor went on for some considerable distance. The passage widened even more as she continued, but it also slanted downward. Riva remembered the tunnel she'd been warned about. So far, it seemed fairly innocuous, other than going on for such a distance. But it appeared to be taking her away from the castle rather than toward it.

Even more disturbing, doors appeared in the sides of the tunnel, rough-hewn, apparently long disused, and closed. They reminded her too forcefully of the dream she'd had of being in a corridor similar to this one.

The light proved to be a torch burning in a wall sconce, the first of a series that shed just enough radiance to let her move swiftly. Dark, closed-in places had always made her nervous. Riva didn't like the idea of traveling underground and wanted to be out of the tunnel as quickly as possible.

Each time she passed one of the doors, she glanced at it warily and hurried by. Her uneasiness grew when she realized light slipped from cracks around some of the doors, suggesting inhabitants beyond those panels. She had no desire to meet any of the residents of this place.

The creaking of rusty hinges from somewhere ahead sent a wave of cold dread pouring through her. What kind of creature would live down here in this dark, isolated corridor? She slowed her pace, but she couldn't stop entirely. It had to be faced. More screeches and creaking suggested other doors, many more. The cold sweat began to run down her temples and under her shirt.

After passing two more closed doors, she approached one that stood open by a few inches. She didn't see or hear anyone as she rushed past it. The next door, just a few feet ahead, was also ajar. A hand protruded from the opening, its fingers wrapped around the wood panel. The flesh on it was withered and clung tightly to long, narrow bones, giving the impression of a skeletal figure.

Riva sucked in a sharp gasp of air. She didn't want to see any more of that creature or any others down here. She rushed forward. The corridor continued — endlessly, it seemed — disappearing into the dim light with no indication of an end. More doors creaked open. Worse yet, whispery, crackling voices spoke softly around her. The sounds echoed off the stone walls and ceiling, but she couldn't distinguish words. It was more of a chorus of rippling vowels.

Doors squealed and groaned open at irregular intervals on either side of the corridor for as far ahead as she could see. Arms followed hands, emerging from the cracks. Inevitably heads poked out as well. Withered, skeletal faces peered out at her, male and female, all with thin layers of flesh clinging tightly to the bones. Some had thin, stringy hair, some were bald. Wide, nearly lidless eyes stared at her as she passed.

Her own breathing grew loud enough to echo around the hall, joining the waves of whispers. Her heart pounded so hard she could hear it throbbing and she shivered in the chilly air. Footsteps sounded behind her. It had to be the figures she'd seen stepping out into the hall and following, but she was too terrified to turn and look.

She didn't need to, anyway. They emerged from doors in front of her as well. She slowed down. Wispy forms floated out into the passage, and every one of them turned her way. Tall, short, thin, round, dark, light, male, female, they came in all the varieties of the human race, but none of them appeared completely alive. Though they moved and spoke in those strange low whispers, no thoughts or emotions animated the eerily expressionless faces. Even some that appeared to be the forms of children showed no emotion.

Riva halted as the creatures gathered in front of and behind her. Terror squeezed her stomach into a tight knot. The horse neighed, pawed at the ground, and tried to pull away from her. She hung onto the reins as the gathering spectral crowd closed in around her. The noise, a low hum of whispers and some deeper groans, grew louder. She still could distinguish no specific words in the torrent.

Her breath caught in her throat and she had to clear it before she could say, "Who are you? What do you want?"

The hum grew louder and even more chaotic before one word emerged clearly from it, *touch*. It was more plea than order.

"Touch? You want to touch me?"

The figures gathered in closer. The hum rose to a buzz that echoed bizarrely down the corridor.

Two words worked their way out of the noise. *You touch*. It was a request rather than a demand.

"You want me to touch you," she ventured.

The wave of hums and whispers rippled and grew, suggesting her answer was the right one. It also contained a wordless plea.

Riva didn't want to do it. She dreaded these creatures with their inanimate expressions and lifeless eyes. The thought of touching them made her almost physically sick.

"I…" At first words refused to make it past the fear that all but strangled her. "I don't think I can. Please, don't ask it."

She expected them to crowd her more closely yet, to demand the touch they wanted, even force her into it, or fall on her with more devastating results. Riva waited for their reaction.

They began to back away. With no expressions on their faces or in the way they carried themselves, she could read no emotion in them. But the sound they made changed, getting lower, softer, more plaintive. They wouldn't demand the touch they requested, she realized, but her refusal grieved them. Something in their sad, mournful hum clutched at her soul. She wondered what would happen if she did touch one, and why they seemed to want it so much.

"Yes. I'll try," she ventured. "One of you. Just one."

Again the humming changed pitch and tone. There was some twitching and turning of the creatures, and then one finally stepped forward from the crowd. A short, bent old man with no hair, no teeth, and round eyes with black irises moved toward her.

Riva drew a deep breath. If this was a test, she had no clue to the right answer. She extended a hand toward the old man until her fingers touched his cheek. It was skin her fingers brushed along, but hard, cold, dead skin.

Nonetheless, a tidal wave of thoughts, emotions, memories, a lifetime of dreams and delusions, hopes and disappointments, rolled over her in a flood that threatened to engulf her. But it was a brief invasion. The outpouring turned off as quickly as it had begun with her touch. Following it was only warmth and gratitude, expressed as pure emotion emanating from the old man. She dropped her fingers from him, and he backed away.

The rest stood around, watching her, humming their mournful, tuneless plea.

Riva stared back at them. Pity and compassion warred with distaste and won. She turned to the nearest woman and beckoned her forward.

The woman should have been in her middle years, had she been alive at all. When she stepped forward, Riva pressed her fingers to the woman's forehead and was again almost overwhelmed by the flood of thoughts and feelings. As before it lasted only a moment, and then was replaced by a soothing warmth, a strange feeling of well-being, before the woman backed away.

One by one, the others came forward at her nod to receive the benediction of contact. Riva had no idea why they wanted this, what it was doing for them, but they clearly craved it and derived something from it, so she continued touching each one in turn, accepting the hemorrhage of mental activity from them, feeling it transmute to peace and acceptance.

After each had received the blessing from her, he or she would move back, standing against the wall of the passage. As there were possibly a hundred or more of them, it took some time to touch each one. Her head ached from all the feelings and thoughts she'd absorbed by the time she did the last one.

When it was done, they all moved back, forming two rows on either side of the corridor, leaving room enough for her to pass down the center.

They still made the low, humming noise, but the pleading tone had changed to one of contentment and peace. Why that should be, she couldn't begin to guess, just as she had no clue what her touch had done for them. But they seemed pleased with her efforts. As she passed by them, another word emerged from the general buzz. It sounded like, *Guide.*

Riva couldn't guess what that meant either, but as it didn't seem to offer any obvious help, she ignored it.

They let her pass between their lines with no further attempt to hinder her. On reaching the end of the group, she turned and looked back. They continued to watch her, humming or buzzing. Unsure what moved her to do so, Riva bowed to them. They bowed in return. Then one of them — an older woman — emerged from the line on her left and came toward her.

"Guide," the woman said. The word was such a low, whispery hum, Riva could barely understand her. The elderly woman was thin to the point of emaciation, and her face just as expressionless as the others. Riva had to fight an urge to draw back when the other reached toward her and took her hand. "Guide," she repeated.

A momentary surge of emotion — bone-deep sorrow and grief — passed from the woman to Riva, then it was cut off as though a door had been slammed shut between them. The woman tugged at Riva's hand, urging her forward.

No more doors appeared in the walls, but there were occasional niches carved into the rock, sometimes with stone statues or incised stone plates set into them. Riva tried to decipher the carving on one plate, but gave up quickly. The light was too low to see clearly, and what she could discern made little sense. The stylized drawings might have represented almost anything.

Behind her, the creaks and squeals of doors opening and closing sounded, but that faded to nothing as they proceeded. After a few minutes of deep silence, broken only by the clop of the horse's hooves and the scraping of her own boots on the rocky floor, she became aware of another sound. Water. Not the plink or gurgle of a small stream falling along the rock, but a rushing torrent.

The light faded as they left behind the last torch. Nothing but darkness loomed ahead. Riva wished she hadn't already used up her only light. Even with the services of her "guide," she desperately feared having to negotiate that passage with no illumination and the possibility of falling into an underground river.

She whispered a spell that should provide a small light. The glow grew from her hand, but rapidly flickered and died out. She tried again with the same result. A third try convinced her something in the tunnel absorbed the magical energy she poured into the light and swallowed it up. There had to be some other way to provide radiance, but nothing occurred to her besides turning back. She hated the oppressive darkness and the helpless feeling it induced in her. Walking blind that way robbed her of breath as well as sight.

It appeared she would have little choice in the matter, other than to retrace her steps and seek another way into the castle. Somehow she doubted there would be any alternative. It seemed clear she was meant to go this way, no matter how much she disliked the idea.

Riva stumbled along in the darkness, trying to take care, but the thin woman tugged at her hand when she lagged too much. Her guide said nothing more, but kept tight hold of her. The horse grew uneasy about the darkness as well, and Riva had to keep pulling him forward.

Her guide either knew the corridor well or was able to see better in the darkness. The woman seemed to have no doubts about the way they should go as she turned them to the left and then slightly to the right. Several times she swerved a bit, as though steering them around unseen obstacles.

The darkness pressed on Riva like an actual weight. Even when her eyes adjusted to it, she could make out nothing of their surroundings. The scrape of her boots and the horse's hooves on the stone floor sounded far too loud. The musty, damp smell of the air nearly overpowered her. More alarmingly, the noise of rushing water had become much louder. They were closer to the torrent.

Riva had to fight a rising sense of panic about being trapped eternally in the stone passages, lost and forgotten, or falling into some underground river. No one knew where she was or would be able to find her. Was she doomed to become one of the emaciated denizens of the corridor? How did they live down here?

If they did live. Though they wore a coating of flesh over their bones, something about their lack of expression or animation led her to think they weren't truly alive in the sense she knew. Since they moved, spoke—sort of—and felt, they couldn't be said to be truly dead, either. She didn't know what they were.

She was quite sure she didn't want to become one of them, any more than she wanted to be trapped in the horrible, echoing, empty darkness. Her "guide" could be leading her anywhere, and Riva had no way to know if she was going the right way or heading for a deep well, the lair of some creature of darkness that would eat her up.

Who would ever know her fate, should that happen? Panic drew a sharp whimper that echoed off the walls of the tunnel as she shivered in the chilly air.

Had she been reduced to that? What was wrong with her? The feeling of being lost with no one knowing where she was, no hope of rescue should something happen, sent waves of cold fear up and down her spine.

Then in the midst of her panic, the images of Daniel and Leinad formed in her mind. Somehow they'd always known where she was or would be. They had cared for her. They expected to see her again and would surely look for her if she didn't appear where they expected. Or would they know that she'd failed and not come looking?

The doubts she'd had about their directions in the last couple of days assailed her yet again. Did they truly want her to succeed? Had they directed her here so she would be thoroughly lost underground where no one would ever find her?

She didn't believe it. They'd suffered for her and made love to her. Leinad had held her with care while they'd punished her, and watched her pain with compassion. They'd shared laughter over their dinners and the deeper, healing joy of the limited lovemaking they'd been allowed.

In her heart she found something else, a realization she'd been avoiding because she couldn't see a way that it wouldn't lead to pain. She was in love with them. Both of them. If it were possible, she would want to spend the rest of her life with them.

She thrilled to everything she'd done with them—even the punishments. Her most secret fantasies included a lover who mastered her and refused to allow her spoiled, willful nature to have its way unanswered. The lovemaking sessions left her breathless with gratitude and joy, if frustrated that they couldn't complete the ultimate fulfillment of their feelings for each other.

It wasn't possible. She had obligations to her family, to win the platter and bring it back to them. They counted on her to bring them the object that would help heal her father and the land. She had to go back and leave Leinad and Daniel behind. In any case, they likely had obligations of their own.

And there were two of them. Her father, the rest of the family, the people of the keep, none would understand her having two men, wanting both of them for husbands. She couldn't choose between them. She loved them both equally, in slightly different ways. One without the other would leave an emptiness, a void. Having neither of them... It would cut her to the heart when she had to say goodbye to them.

The pain seared into her, but it also reassured her. Daniel and Leinad would not ignore her or let her death go unremarked. Perhaps they'd even help her get out. Was it possible that the woman leading her through the darkness, cautioning her with a squeeze about uneven ground, was their way of assisting?

Her panic receded, though her discomfort with the chilly darkness and fear of the water rushing nearby continued to plague her. The journey went on for a long time, until finally they came to a place where her guide stopped and said, very softly, "Bridge. Cross here."

Riva couldn't see it. In the oppressive blackness, she couldn't discern the edges of the bridge or the water now running beneath them. The rush of the torrent made an overwhelming roar, however, and served to further disorient her. She had to rely on her guide to keep them on the span. It was one of the hardest things she'd ever done. But she kept putting one foot in front of the other, following the woman's lead until she could tell by the changed footing beneath that they were on the far side of the river. The horse clopped along behind her, making it clear he wasn't happy about the situation, but trusting her guidance.

"Go on, now," the woman whispered. "Light soon." She took Riva's hand and placed it against the wall of the passage, then released her hold. Before Riva had realized what was happening, her guide was gone. She moved so silently Riva had no idea which way she'd departed.

"Thank you for your help," she called, unsure whether the woman would hear or care.

Chapter Nineteen

It still took an effort of will to move forward. Not much farther on, though, she saw the pale glow of a light ahead. It proved to be a torch in a wall mount. Who kept the torches refreshed and burning down here? Those emaciated, semi-alive creatures who'd wanted her to touch them? Whoever it was had her heartfelt gratitude.

She drew in a deep breath and let it out on a long sigh of relief.

The tunnel continued for some distance. Three more burning torches illuminated a plain corridor, just wide enough and high enough for the horse to pass easily. There were no doors or other openings along this stretch.

Riva walked for fifteen or twenty minutes before she saw another, different light in the distance. It was brighter and more yellow/orange, suggesting actual daylight.

Heartened by the thought of finally emerging from this horrible passage, she hurried forward, almost running as the increasing glow convinced her there was indeed an exit ahead. The horse seemed nearly as heartened as she was and happily trotted along with her.

At the end of the tunnel, a wide arch opened out into a broad swath of manicured grass with a few trees scattered around the area. Late afternoon sunshine flowed toward her, warming her, driving away the chill that had settled into her bones underground.

Only when she'd actually emerged from the passage and moved beyond a short corridor of trees, could she tell that she was in a broad courtyard that appeared to be at the back of the castle. The huge mass of the keep was on her right. A round tower rose on either side of it. When she looked back, she realized the arch emerged from the wall itself. Had she been inside or beneath the wall for the entire trip? It appeared it was likely so. From the position of the sun, she deduced she'd circled the keep on the west side and come out at the back of it, on the north.

A broad path led from the tunnel's exit, curving past several smaller structures, toward a door in the side of the keep. Riva set off toward the castle. The sun still shone brightly and she basked in its warmth and light.

One of the buildings she passed had its broad, wide doors standing open, giving a view of a series of stalls. A few horses occupied some of them. Nearby a man mucked out one of the empty spaces. He stopped when he saw her, set aside the shovel, and came to the door.

A huge smile spread across a face that could only generously be described as homely. "You're here, at last. We've been waiting for you. Bring your horse in. We'll take care of him. You can't take him into the castle, you know."

"How did you know I was coming?"

He shrugged and his smile crooked. "I canna tell ye that, lady. 'Tis just that we know." He turned to the horse and began running his hands over its neck and down its flanks. "Ye're a beauty, ye are," he crooned to the horse. "I have some nice fresh hay for ye."

The horse seemed to enjoy the attention. Riva took her pack and slung it over her shoulder. She waited, watching, while the man led the animal back to a stall. A desolate feeling poured over her, as though she'd suddenly lost an old friend.

The man turned to stare at her. "Yer horse will be cared for as well as I know how." His grin split even wider. "And I do know how very well, though it may not behoove me to say so. Off with ye, now. There's still a trial or two to go, and they be a waiting for ye'. It's taken ye long enough."

Sighing, Riva turned and left the stable, heading for the castle. It was a short walk to the single step that led up to the back of the keep. The door guarding the entrance was clearly not one used for honored guests or important visitors. A plain, unadorned wood panel had a lever handle, but no bell or knocker. A small, hand-lettered sign tacked to the wood said, "Admit Yourself."

She drew a deep breath and pushed on the latch. The mechanism clicked and the door swung inward. The small anteroom beyond the entrance appeared to be deserted. Riva stepped in and immediately noted how quiet it was. If anyone was anywhere about, she could detect no sign of it. A rough table and a coat rack comprised all the furnishings. Neither held anything beyond a light coating of dust. Two corridors led from the room on either side of her. No one showed up to greet her or give directions, even after she'd waited for some time.

Finally, she looked around, debating which corridor was more likely to take her wherever she was supposed to be going. In doing so, she noted a pair of small signs on the walls. Each one bore nothing but an arrow drawn in red. One pointed toward the corridor on the right, and the other pushed toward the alternate way. Perhaps either route would get her to her destination.

Riva looked at both corridors and arbitrarily chose the one on her right.

It went on for some ways with no openings other than a few high windows that provided illumination. After spending so long leading the horse, it felt odd not to have it trailing along behind her or worrying about whether or not it could fit through narrow openings. At least there was enough light here to let her easily see the way.

The hall she traversed made a sharp right hand bend. Before she'd gone more than twenty feet or so, another open arch offered the option to go to the left. To her surprise there was another sign tacked to the wall just inside the arch. An arrow on it pointed in the direction of the corridor to the left.

Presuming the arrows were meant to signal the correct route for her to get to wherever she was supposed to end up inside the castle, Riva turned that way. The corridor soon made another left-hand turn into a small boxy room. For a moment, Riva thought there was another person coming to meet her. The other woman seemed jarringly familiar for a disjointed moment, until she recognized herself and realized there must be a mirror ahead.

Her surety was short-lived. The woman ahead turned slightly away from her as she approached. When she was close enough to touch the smooth, cool surface of the glass, Riva's confusion and doubts grew.

Behind the woman in the mirror was not the expected dark, plain walls of the corridors she traversed, but a furnished room, one that looked remarkably like her own quarters in the castle at home.

The scene changed and the woman disappeared, though the room remained the same. The chamber was undoubtedly her own. A young girl—herself when she was no more than eight or nine—lay in the bed, surrounded by several people.

She remembered the occasion well enough. Though she'd had a generally healthy childhood, on that day she'd been quite sick. Knowing it was entirely her own fault made it no less miserable. The cook and two scullery maids had warned her against eating too much of the trifle and cream prepared for that evening's dinner. But Riva had always heeded her own will above anyone else's advice, and she'd eaten far more of the sweet than was wise, with the result that she was very sick the next day. Sadly, both the cook and the maids had been punished for allowing her to eat too much. As if they could have stopped her.

Her stomach clenched again. Though she'd been a child at the time, she saw now the seeds of a willful, spoiled young woman sprouting. She wished she could go back and apologize to those who'd suffered for her selfishness.

Riva retraced her steps for a little ways, but halted where a corridor branched off to the left. A sign posted on the wall nearby pointed that way. She didn't remember seeing it when she'd approached from the other direction, but perhaps it hadn't been as visible from that side. She rounded the corner indicated, entering another plain, dimly lit corridor. It stopped at a blank wall, but a passage went off to the right, so she followed it.

Two corridors exited to the left. They had no signs pointing toward them, so Riva continued forward. Before long a dim reflection of herself showing ahead warned her as she approached another mirror. As before, though, the reflection changed as she drew closer, shifting from being her own reflection to that of herself at an earlier age.

The setting was the same as the previous scene, her own chambers in the castle, but the events she saw were from several years later, when she'd been around fifteen or sixteen. Her governess and her father were in the background. The older woman had tears in her eyes.

Riva had balked at her needlework lessons and argued with her governess constantly. She'd finally gone to her father and complained, and the governess had been released from her duties.

Riva wondered what the woman was doing now. She'd left the area soon after her dismissal, and they had no idea where she'd gone. Riva hadn't liked her overmuch, but the woman was more annoying than evil. She probably hadn't deserved to be summarily dismissed.

Another piece of her past she'd change if she could. Not that she'd keep Elaine on as governess, but she'd insist that another, comparable position be found for her.

Sighing, Riva turned away. She really wasn't happy to have this indictment of her past being thrown at her this way, but she supposed it was another test.

More signs directed her along a series of turns and down several sets of corridors. She kept watch for the next mirror. Surely there was more she needed to see. Already she was getting the drift, she was self-centered and willful. Her father had indulged her far too much, especially after her mother had died, which had happened just a year after Lia's birth.

Three turns later, the expected mirror waited at the end of the passage. Riva approached it unhappily.

The woman in the mirror didn't fade out this time, but only changed subtly. This was surely herself again, but a slightly younger version, as though the glass showed her as she was two or three years ago, when she'd been thinner and her hair was longer. Her image turned away from the mirror and spoke to someone else in the room. When she moved a bit, Riva saw her sister, Lia, in the background. Lia wore an elaborate pink gown over a shift cut daringly low in the front. Riva remembered the occasion.

They'd all been invited to a ball given by the Baron d'Esterville, and their father had ordered new gowns for each of them. Lia was excited about finally being considered adult enough to be included. Unfortunately, she'd had their needlewomen make her dress much more daring than was proper. Riva had to tell her she would need to get it fixed. Lia didn't take it well.

Looking at the scene as it unfolded yet again in the mirror, Riva realized several things she hadn't—but should have—at the time.

Lia had been intensely proud of her new grown-up status as she paraded into the room in the gown. She'd never before worn anything so grand or glamorous or flattering. She did look lovely in the gown—too much so. Riva worried she would attract too much of the wrong sort of attention as well as offending propriety. And she herself had not been as kind and tactful in telling her sister as she might have been. Her criticism had devastated Lia.

Looking at the scene rolling over again, Riva wished she had it to do over. She could have been so much more gentle, so much nicer about it. She could have made the point without reducing Lia to angry words and tears.

Riva turned away, fighting tears herself. It hurt her soul to see the pain she'd inflicted on her sister that day, all the more so because Lia had quickly forgiven her, gotten the gown redone, and made no further fuss. But Lia hadn't shown it — or several other gowns she'd had made since — to her sister before she wore them.

Riva sighed again. She had many regrets but could do nothing to change the past. Should she survive this, though, she would certainly not be the same person she would have been, had she never come to the island.

She backed away, wondering if there were any more scenes she needed to see. The message had certainly been delivered.

Whoever had set up the maze apparently agreed, since she encountered no more mirrors. Two turns and one long corridor later, she came to a place where she had to choose one of three possible passages. A sign over one said, "No regrets." Over the second it said, "Regrets Only." The sign over the third read, "Regrets and Atonement."

She paused and considered, though she knew immediately which one she ought to take. Worry over what "atonement" might mean made her hesitate for a moment, but she screwed up her courage and went that way.

Another long corridor stretched ahead of her, went around a bend, and finally ended in a set of large double doors. A faint hum of human voices in conversation sounded from beyond them. Riva stopped there, wondering about her next move. Should she go right in? Knock? Announce herself? There was no sign above the portal to help her decide. She worked up her nerve again and pushed open the right-side door.

Chapter Twenty

An enormous chamber opened out in front of her, lined with rows of grand pillars supporting the roof, leading toward a dais on which several people sat. The room was crowded with people, most in grand, courtly dress.

The buzz of conversation stopped at her entry as everyone turned to look her way. Surprised and puzzled, Riva halted, studying the situation. Compared to the finely groomed, well-dressed members of the crowd, she felt grimy, weary, and travel-stained.

"Come here, child," a voice called from the far end of the room. It belonged to the same older woman she'd met in her dream vision the night Daniel and Leinad had been punished. "Approach. We've awaited your arrival."

Riva drew herself up, reminding herself that, no matter her appearance, she was a princess. Giving no hint of embarrassment, she marched down the long hall toward the dais. As she approached, she looked at the other people sitting on the platform. Surprise almost made her halt for a moment when she saw Leinad and Daniel among them, seated on one end. They both wore deep blue velvet, embroidered with gold filigree, over fawn leggings and white linen shirts. Daniel's mouth crooked just a bit, but Leinad smiled openly and warmly at her.

The older woman who sat in the center of the dais also smiled on her.

Behind the woman, a series of small silver platters sat on edge on a narrow shelf, facing out. In the center was a larger platter, the one she'd seen her first night on the island.

Riva halted at the foot of the dais. "My lady," she said, bowing.

"Princess Riva of Serendonia," the woman greeted her. "I'm D'Jillan, the Keeper of this island. We welcome you here. Your journey has been long and hard, and you're weary. Soon you'll have rest. But first there is one more test you must face."

The old woman paused. "You've done well since your first mistake, and we honor you for your success. We also honor your fellow questers who've helped and guided you in this." She nodded toward Leinad and Daniel. "Based on your last choice, you've learned a great deal on this journey." Her eyebrows rose slightly. "Should you be wondering, the atonement you chose will come, but later. For now, there are other things we must consider."

She paused, sighed lightly, and nodded toward the end of the dais. Daniel and Leinad both rose, stepped down from the dais, and came toward her. Riva smiled at them but was surprised to see Daniel's expression had turned grim, while Leinad's look showed both compassion and a tinge of fear. Her pleasure in seeing them faded into doubt. What would be demanded of her now?

"Princess," D'Jillan addressed her again. "I see you still carry your sword. I presume you're trained in its use?"

"I am, Lady D'Jillan."

"Excellent. I would ask you to draw it now, please, Princess."

Though she wondered what test might require the use of her sword, she did as D'Jillan requested and pulled it from the scabbard. She held it in a relaxed, ready position.

Riva looked up and met D'Jillan's cool, gray eyes.

"I believe you were warned you would at some time be asked to do something that would seem completely outrageous, even terrible, to you," the woman said. "That time has come." She nodded to Leinad and Daniel.

They stepped toward her and D'Jillan moved back.

Leinad's voice wobbled a little bit when he said, "Princess Riva, I must ask you to make a choice. You must choose between Daniel and myself." He drew a deep breath. "You must use your sword to slay one of us. Your choice is which one of us will live."

Shock froze her in place. Riva dropped the sword. The loud clang as it hit the floor didn't distract her attention, which wavered between Leinad and Daniel. For long moments, she could say nothing at all. Even when she was able to speak, she had difficulty forcing out anything coherent. "You can't...You can't mean that. It's... How can I decide? How can I slay either of you? You must know I love you both. I cannot harm you."

Daniel nodded grimly. "'Tis for love of us that you must slay one or the other. More than that I cannot say."

Leinad added, "As you love us, and we do love you as well, I beg that you trust us and do as we ask."

Riva bent to pick up the sword, hoping the action would give her a minute to control the tears that had begun to spill down her face. She couldn't believe what they asked her to do. She'd never taken a human life with her sword. She wasn't at all sure she could bring herself to slay anyone.

Her eyes burned as she straightened up again. "I must truly do this?" She hoped, prayed someone would tell her it was but a jest. "I must choose between you and slay one? It cannot be. I can*not* do it."

Leinad drew a deep breath. "Princess, I can say little as to reasons, but only ask that you believe when I assure you there is one. I beg you trust us and do as you're asked."

She nodded, but added, "How do I choose? How do I know which of you I must slay?"

"You must use your judgment in that, my lady," Leinad answered. "We trust you to make the right decision."

"I know not how. What sort of test can this be that asks me to do so foul a deed? 'Tis wrong! I will not do it."

Leinad moved closer to her and laid his paws on her shoulders. "Princess, I cannot tell you all the reasons, but what we ask of you is not wrong—just hard. As you love us, please do as we ask. 'Tis a terrible thing, I know, but so it must be."

She had a hard time focusing on his face through the tears, but she met his golden brown eyes and saw the plea in them. Her heart broke as she nodded. "You truly wish me to do this?" She silently begged him to tell her nay.

"Aye, Princess," he answered. "We *need* you to do it. You must."

D'Jillan intervened to say, "Princess, you've been trained to believe that the taking of any human life is evil, and that is not wrong. Yet, I tell you that in this instance, 'tis not wrong. 'Tis necessary and right. How it may be so cannot be obvious to you, and I cannot as yet tell you. You must make the choice and do as you're bid if you wish to complete your quest. Only one spirit and one body can continue. One spirit must be freed from its current container of flesh, one body freed of the spirit currently within."

Riva felt as though she were breaking apart into a thousand small pieces. How could she decide between them and kill one? Who was she to decide which one of them would live and which one die? But the burden had been put on her, and she no idea how to choose or where she would find the strength to do this thing.

Riva raised her sword but held it so it pointed between them. Which one of them? Daniel was beautiful in face and body and showed occasional signs of warmth despite his somewhat dour personality. On the other hand, despite his ugly face and beast's claws and fur, Leinad was warm, kind, and gentle. How did she choose between them?

Was she supposed to decide which of them deserved more to live? How could she make such a judgment?

She couldn't.

She had to.

She couldn't.

She had to.

Riva raised the sword again and stared at Daniel, then at Leinad. Neither said anything nor seemed concerned about his possible impending death.

Why not?

What did they know that she didn't? Had D'Jillan given her a hint with the words about freeing one spirit?

She considered Daniel's and Leinad's resemblance to each other and their names that were the reverse of each other, and she began to understand.

It didn't answer the most pressing question, though. Which spirit cried out to be freed? Which body should continue, free of the spirit currently within?

But she knew, or thought she knew, little though she liked what it meant.

Every instinct in her cried against the deed. Yet D'Jillan, Leinad and Daniel assured her it was right.

Praying she'd made the right choice, Riva sucked in a deep breath, lunged forward, and buried her sword in Leinad's chest.

Chapter Twenty-One

She watched the expression on his kind, ugly face change to shock and surprise and then into pain. Within moments, though, a look of peace and even contentment settled across his misshapen features. His eyes were wide and watched her steadily, even as his body folded up and began to sink to the floor.

Riva drew her sword back out of his chest, bracing herself for the spurt of blood that would follow.

It didn't. Riva stared at her sword. Not even a small red smear marked its gleaming surface.

Nor did any blood spill from the wound. She stared at his chest, uncomprehending. The sword had penetrated nearly all the way through him. How could there be no blood?

Riva dropped the sword on the floor and sank to her knees beside Leinad's prone body. She drew his head onto her lap, brushing her hand across the fur on his face. He still watched her.

"You chose rightly, Princess," he said, the words a bare whisper. Then he smiled at her and died.

Around her, people spoke in hushed, respectful tones. D'Jillan rested her hands on Riva's shoulders, patting her as Riva broke down into huge, heaving sobs.

Moments later, astonishment stopped the tears and stilled her shaking.

As soon as the animation left Leinad's face, his body began to fade, the mass of him simply disappearing from sight. Within moments naught remained of him but the misty outline of a man. No flesh, no fur, no blood, no bone, just moving air and the faint remnants of form and features. His spirit or ghost rose from the floor and turned slowly until it faced the form of Daniel. Everyone in the room watched in silence as what remained of Leinad walked toward the other man.

Riva rose to her feet and sucked in a sharp breath as the spirit walked right *into* Daniel, the moving outline blending with the flesh and blood of the living man. Daniel shut his eyes, his face drawn into tight lines of pain. His breath came heavy and hard, and his fists clenched tight against his chest.

For long moments, there was no sound in the room, as everyone's attention focused on Daniel's struggle. It was a strange, silent battle, with only the changing expression on the man's face showing the war going on within. Riva could only guess at what forces were arrayed on either side and what the cost to the living man.

She took a step toward him, but D'Jillan put an arm out to stop her.

No one else moved or made a sound.

Agonizingly long moments passed before the look of pain and struggle began to fade from Daniel's face. He opened his eyes, sucked in a huge breath, and the tension drained from his body. His fists relaxed, the rigid set of his shoulders eased, he reached up and ran a hand through his hair, looked down at his fingers, then looked back up and smiled.

His smile was the most beautiful sight Riva had ever seen. It made his brown eyes glow with molten gold sparks and combined the beauty of Daniel's face and form with the sweetness and strength of Leinad's spirit.

D'Jillan moved from Riva's side, approaching Daniel. "Who are you?" she asked him.

"I'm Daniel," he said, making the name two syllables this time instead of the three they'd been dividing the name into. "Daniel of Winterose."

"You are whole now," D'Jillan said.

"Aye." He looked at the Keeper, then his gaze moved around the room until he found Riva. "With gratitude to Princess Riva."

D'Jillan stepped back, allowing Daniel to move to stand in front of her.

"Lady," he said, "I can never thank you for all you've done and for being who you are, a woman with enough strength and courage and love to pass the island's tests and make me whole." His golden brown eyes, the eyes of her dream-lover, studied her with gratitude and—she hoped—love.

"I owe you much for making it possible," she told him. "You helped me gain another chance when I failed, you guided me on the right way, punished me as needed, and loved me more than I deserved." She reached toward him to brush hair back from his face, but lost her nerve and dropped the hand to her side.

"Less than you deserved, lady. And do not discount what you have done for me. My failure in the quest was far worse than yours." He drew a deep breath as though he still found it difficult to discuss. "I attempted to take the platter without earning it. I, too, was granted a second chance, but my punishment meant being split into two people, one of them a seeming monster. Only in assisting another quester to successfully complete the island's tests, and then having her slay one of my seemings, could I be made whole again."

He reached for the hand she'd dropped to her side and took it between both of his. "I was gifted more than I deserved that you came here to free me. Your love lent you the strength to do what seemed a terrible deed." He lifted the hand he'd taken to his mouth and kissed her palm.

Riva shivered as his lips caressed her flesh. It sent familiar tingles of desire running through her.

"Princess Riva, Lord Daniel." D'Jillan spoke, drawing their attention back to her. She moved to the foot of the dais, stepped up, and reached up to take a pair of platters from the shelf.

"Approach, both of you," she ordered.

Hand in hand, Riva and Daniel moved to the foot of the dais.

D'Jillan handed each of them one of the small, silver plates. "You have each fulfilled the tests and trials of your quest for the silver platter. As you see, though, there is not just one silver platter, but many, and each has the properties legend attributes to them. Take your platters. I have no doubt you will each use them wisely."

The crowd of people that had watched the drama play out broke into sudden applause. It startled Riva, who'd been so immersed in the interaction with Daniel and D'Jillan, she'd forgotten others were present.

D'Jillan moved closer to them, and under cover of the noise, added, "I hope you two will find your paths run together. Your love for each other is beyond the ordinary, and I honor it. I give you also these gifts to help you. First, at your request, you'll be shown a way to travel rapidly to your own lands, by using certain special gates we know. These will be available to you for your use for the rest of your lives. Thus you may quickly and easily spend time with each of your families and fulfill whatever promises have been made to them."

She smiled at them, noting the glances they shared. "This also I give you. For short periods of time, no more than an hour a week, Daniel may, at his will, split himself into his two former seemings of Leinad and Daniel." The woman looked at Riva. "I believe you might find this pleasing to you, Princess?" Her look was arch and suggestive.

"Aye, my lady," Riva answered, wondering suddenly how much D'Jillan knew of their interactions. Another set of doubts assailed her. Despite her words, Riva didn't know, in truth, whether it would benefit her, as she knew not whether Daniel wanted a future with her.

Daniel looked at her, and his smile set her pulse racing. "I do think it will please her, my lady, "Daniel said to D'Jillan, though his gaze remained on Riva. "I hope it will. I hope we'll have many occasions to enjoy this gift. Especially if..."

He lifted her hand again. "Lady Riva, would you do me the honor of consenting to be my lady wife?" Instead of waiting for an answer, he continued, "I realize you know naught of my family, which is of the nobility, though not royalty as is your own, nor know you aught of my background and nature. Yet do I hope you know enough of my character to believe we would be well matched." He drew her closer. "I love you more than my life as well," he said more quietly.

Riva wanted to throw herself in his arms. She needed to learn how this melding of Leinad and Daniel into one man would work. She had no doubt that it would, but the differences would require some adjustment.

"Lord Daniel, I will. With joy." More softly she added, "I love you as well. At least I have learned to love both Leinad and Daniel, and since both are you, I believe I shall love you even more than either."

He leaned over to kiss her. His lips were warm and tender on hers, and the contact sent tingling waves of need spreading through her. He drew her closer, pressing her against the heat of his long body. She wanted to lose herself in him, especially when she felt the hardness of his arousal and his tongue probed into her mouth.

Before they could get carried away, however, D'Jillan said, "Excuse me." A few people in the room laughed or coughed in embarrassment. The Keeper continued, "I realize you want time alone together, but first there is a banquet prepared to celebrate your success. Will you come join us?"

They drew apart reluctantly. "Aye, my lady," Daniel answered.

Daniel maintained his hold on Riva's hand as they followed D'Jillan into an enormous dining hall. Afterward Riva would not be able to say what she ate that evening. She vaguely remembered platters of savory meats, herb-scented bread, bowls of spiced vegetables, a fruity wine, and afterward a smooth, sweet pudding. Mostly, though, she remembered the feel of Daniel's hand on hers, the touch of his thigh against her leg, the way they smiled at each other like two silly children each time their eyes met.

Toasts were made and speeches given in their honor, but later she could remember nothing of them.

She ate well enough to satisfy her hunger, but her mind barely noticed. She talked to D'Jillan and Daniel about her home, her family, and her lands, and she listened to Daniel speak about his. They agreed to take the platter to her family first, then quickly visit his family before returning to her home to make preparations for their wedding. Riva looked forward to introducing Daniel to her father, brother, and sister.

Musicians played a set of lively, spirited tunes, accompanying a performing group that demonstrated several complicated rounds and step dances. Then everyone else joined the dancing. As they moved up and down in the line dances, she and Daniel joined hands and glances. His golden brown eyes held smoldering lights, and she thought she could lose herself in them. Occasionally she forgot the moves as she drowned in the pleasure of watching him. He was such a miracle—this strong, handsome, warm-hearted man she loved to distraction. And he loved her.

The music changed to a slower, more romantic tune, and couples paired off individually. She moved into the arms of her lover. His hand rested warm on her side and his breath whispered across her ear. They danced together easily and naturally, their motions meshing as though they read each other's thoughts and intentions. His body was warm against hers and his erect cock jabbed into her as they moved. To have that much power over him that she could evoke this physical need...bliss. Unadulterated, almost unbearable joy spread through her in such force she wondered if her body could contain it.

She moved in a haze of timeless unreality, drifting in a world that contained only the two of them.

Eventually the celebration ended and people drifted off to their quarters.

Guides showed Daniel and Riva to a pair of richly appointed bedchambers, complete with a private door between them, and tubs full of hot water waiting in either room. It disappointed Riva to bathe separately from him, but she luxuriated in the hot water after the long stressful day. Several attendants helped her scrub down, wash her hair, dry herself, and squirm into a fine, linen shift. They tucked her into bed and left.

Moments after they'd departed, the door creaked lightly and Daniel entered. He wore a richly embroidered robe. "Riva?" he said softly.

She kicked off the bedclothes and went to him. He wrapped her in his arms and trailed hot kisses over her mouth, cheeks, temples, and down her throat. She melted into his embrace, working her hands into the opening of the robe to rest on the flesh of his chest, savoring the feel and the clean, masculine scent of him. He whispered to her about how beautiful he found her and how much he adored her.

Love and fear combined to make her cling to him. The reality of their change of fortunes hadn't sunk in far enough to make her truly believe they had a future together, that this amazing man could adore her so much. Perhaps he had some similar feeling. For a long time they simply held onto each other, running hands over bare flesh to assure themselves they were both real, relishing the sparks that jumped between them. Her body came alive, with heat rushing through her and a fire of longing making her cunt swell.

He backed away, breaking the contact long enough to lift the shift, pull it over her head, toss it aside, and pull her with him to the bed. For a while he sat with her on his lap, stroking her breasts, kissing and nipping at the tips, while his cock pressed into her hip.

After a while of that, when the heat poured through her body in waves and moisture gathered in her swollen cunt, he moved her aside and stood up. She wanted to cling to him, to refuse to let him go, but she would do as he wished.

"Kneel," he said, pointing at the floor beside the bed. When she'd done so, he continued, "Remain here a moment. I'll be back forthwith. There is still the matter of the atonement you owe."

Riva sucked in a hard breath of combined excitement and fear. Part of her wanted to beg him to skip it for now, to put off whatever atonement was owed for another time. Yet she also remembered how excited some of the punishments she'd suffered earlier had left her, the way they built the heat and desire to excruciating levels.

He went back to the other room and returned moments later. He'd left the robe behind and was now completely nude. Riva knew she could easily spend a lifetime contemplating the beauty of his form, the grace of strong muscle over long bones.

When she saw what he carried, she moaned and shivered. All too well, she remembered the fierce bite of the leather strap and the excitement of the pain mingling with her arousal.

The first slap of the leather on her bottom was sharp and stinging. It burned, but the thrill of it worked its way all through her and settled in her loins. Several more strokes followed, leaving ribbons of fire across her derriere and the tops of her thighs. She gasped at the harder strokes, but accepted the pain, trying to absorb it. She missed being able to hold onto Leinad, but with D'Jillan's gift, she'd have that comfort in the future.

He spanked her with the leather, hitting just sharply enough to burn, for several more strokes. Riva dug her fingers into the bedcovers and jumped each time the strap bit. She'd forgotten already how much it hurt, much more than she'd expected, but it was even more exciting than she'd remembered. She moaned aloud when a harder slap poured a river of fire across her bottom. Unable to keep still, she rose from the kneeling position and leaned over the bed, breathing hard as the sting worked its way into every corner of her body.

She barely heard the small clatter when Daniel dropped the strap and came to her. She gasped again, though, when his arm came around her and lifted and lowered her to lay face down on the bed. Gentle hands caressed the sore flesh of her bottom. His tongue traced soothingly along the hot welts. He parted the fleshy cheeks and ran a finger down along the crack, sliding into the sensitive slit, already swollen and wet, weeping for him.

His other arm came around her and brushed across her breasts, fingers circling the tips until she was moaning with the excitement. Tension mounted in her as he found every sensitive, needy fold of flesh on her body. She quivered under his attention.

"Please," she begged. "I need you. In me."

Daniel flipped her over. He kissed her face, her throat, her breasts and down along her belly to her cunt. His tongue worked into the cleft until he found her clit. She bucked and squealed when he licked it and squeezed it between his lips. She screamed when he bit down gently, scraping his teeth along it.

"Daniel," she sobbed. "Now. Please. Inside."

He nodded and shifted until he lay over her, his body pressed against her, his full, hard cock squeezed between their bellies. Her bottom burned where it rubbed against the linens. Her clit throbbed from his kisses.

She looked up at him, losing herself in the loving gaze of his golden brown eyes. She brushed her palms up and down the smooth skin of his back. A part of her expected some fur, but wasn't disappointed not to find any. Now, finally, she would have him, all of him, be joined to him in the most intimate and satisfying way.

"Are you ready, my love?" he asked. "As 'tis your first time, it may be hard."

"I'm ready for you. More than ready."

He shifted. His cock probed at her slit and found the opening. She strained against him, desperate to have him inside. He pushed into her. There was some burn as he stretched her, then a sharper pain as he met the barrier of her maidenhead. A hard lunge and he broke through. She gasped at the sting of it.

He stopped and waited for her to adjust to him, tenderly tracing the line of her throat down to her breast with his fingers. After a few minutes, Riva stirred, inviting him to continue. He pulled back and pushed forward, watching her reaction. Reassured, he began to pump in and out, gasping as the tension tightened his muscles.

His cock touched a spot within that gave her a jolt of pleasure. His balls slapped against her as he pumped in and out. She answered his low moan with a groan of her own. Their accelerating breath mingled. Riva dug her fingers into his back as her body drew into a knot of tension, climbing to a height of pleasure she'd never before reached.

He moved faster and faster. When she thought she could bear no more, that she'd break or fly apart, he stopped, drew back, and plunged harder and deeper. A cry tore from him as his seed spilled into her.

At the same time, she felt the tense knot inside her explode into pieces, coming apart in a huge jolt of pleasure that took her to places she'd never been. It rolled her with peaks of joy and valleys of peace. Beyond exhaustion, beyond the trials of the day, beyond decisions and agonizing choices, she drifted in a place where waves of pleasure continued to crest and break inside her. She clung to the man she loved, ecstatic in the closeness with him, drowning in the knowledge of a future to be shared.

Together they rode the tide of pleasure and its aftermath. They drifted in the most exquisite peace, content for a long time to be in each other's arms, joined in heart, mind, and body.

Riva had known she needed a strong, dominant man, but had never truly believed she'd find one. That he was also a courageous, kind, handsome man, very much the stuff of her dream fantasies, was a gift beyond anything she could possibly have earned. She stroked his long, smooth back to convince herself he was real.

Daniel roused himself after a while and looked at her with concern. "My love," he asked, "are you well enough?"

"Nay, my lord. I am not well enough. I'm far beyond well *enough*. I'm very well indeed. I'm in a heaven I never knew existed and I now never wish to leave."

He sighed and nuzzled at her neck. "I can't promise you 'twill always be heaven, my love," he said. "But 'twill always be an adventure of one sort or another. And we'll face all obstacles together."

"Together," she sighed as his tongue worked its unique magic on a breast. "I do like the sound of that."

"As do I. I've waited for you a long time, and I know now 'twas worth every minute. But…as we're now free to have each other as often as we wish, I'd rather not wait much longer for our second joining. If you think you can bear it."

She turned to him and pushed him back down on the bed. "I can bear it. But first, if it pleases you, there are many things you've not allowed me to do to you e'er this. I understand now why 'twas necessary, but as there are no restrictions now…" She knelt beside him. "I would know more of the taste and feel of you, as you've learned the taste and feel of me."

Her tongue explored him from neck to thighs, swirling over the hard nub of his nipples and around the muscles of his chest, along his abdomen, dipping into his belly button, then continuing down until she reached the hard length of his cock. He groaned when she licked along it. His fingers dug into the bedclothes and held on tight when she took the entire length of it into her mouth. It throbbed against her in an intriguing and arousing way.

He tolerated it with sobbing, panting breaths for a few minutes, then gently pushed her off. "In you. Now," he insisted.

He drove into her hard, but contained his strength, and waited until he felt her quiver with her own incipient climax before he allowed his own to explode.

Eventually they slept, wrapped in each other's arms. And in the morning, they said goodbye to D'Jillan and set out, with their platters, to her father's kingdom.

Enjoy this excerpt from

Bronzequest

Glimmer Quest

© *Copyright Katherine Kingston, 2005*

Riva bent forward to kiss his cheek, then stood up. "That's all the help I can give you, save to repeat that I believe you can do this."

When she left, the room seemed very empty indeed, despite the clutter of packs assembled for the journey, the piles of clothes left, the arms he'd scattered as he tried to decide what to take. He prepared for bed and lay down, hoping sleep would come.

He tossed and turned for a long time, running all sorts of imaginary tests and trials through his head. The journey might be so long he'd be an old man before he found his destination. He might die on the way. Demons might attack. Or wild beasts. He could get lost or fail the tests and die. So many bad outcomes. So few good ones.

Whether what happened next was dream or vision, he couldn't tell.

As he slipped into the half-dozing state that precedes sleep, the shape of a woman formed, materializing against a dark, rough backdrop that might be the mouth of a cave, a black hall or the side of a stone cliff, but almost certainly wasn't the tapestry-hung wall of his room.

She was long and lean, slender, but with full breasts and rounded hips. The only light on the scene came from the figure herself. Pale radiance glowed from her lush, bare, white body. Long, midnight-dark hair rippled with some unfelt breeze, while her eyes, a dark, dark blue, stared straight at him with implacable intensity. Reddish glints shone from the depths of them. Breasts and hips formed perfect, graceful curves that demanded mens' worship. She had an uncanny loveliness, but the ferocity of her expression filled him with dread. When her lips curved into a small, cruel smile, it did nothing to soften the terrible visage. Or its wicked beauty. Her small, white teeth all ended in sharp points.

His body reacted immediately, stiffening with longing. A longing he would deny with every particle of his being, had he any choice.

"Come to me," she said, holding shapely white arms out toward him. "You're mine."

He lay on the bed and couldn't retreat, but if he could have pressed himself down into the mattress any harder he would have.

Her body swayed and drifted with fluid grace as she took two steps toward him. "You fear me. Yet your journey will bring you to me."

He wanted to deny it, but the sounds stuck in his throat. This had to be an effort to frighten him into abandoning his quest. Surely.

She drifted closer to him. "We have so much to learn. Let me show you what I have for you." Her voice, low and hoarse, rasped in his ears.

"Who are you?" The words felt dragged out of him. He didn't even know if he spoke them aloud or just in his head.

She heard. "I'm your destiny. I'm what you most want and most fear." She hovered over him. He tried to roll over to avoid her, but his body refused to answer the demand and remained frozen in place, unable to move at all save to breathe and blink.

"I'm your greatest challenge. Pleasure and pain, lady and whore. I'm what you want more than life itself and fear even more."

A pale hand, with long, white fingers, reached forward and touched his face. The feel of it sent a jolt like a lightning bolt through him. The touch burned with a deep, fiery pain, yet it lit his insides with need.

"I'm your dream and your nightmare. The one you long for and the one you dread."

"No." The word came out on a bare wisp of air and lacked conviction.

A smile curved her ripe, red lips. "You say 'no' and mean 'yes'."

He tried to shake his head, to deny it.

"You want me. Will you give yourself to me?"

His mouth refused to shape the words of denial that sprang to his tongue.

She ran pale, cool fingers down his cheek. Fire and ice touched him, drove into him. It burned both hot and cold. The sensation grew until he didn't know if he could bear it without screaming. Yet pleasure, deep and rich, almost brutally strong, mixed in with the pain. She lifted her hand from him and it stopped. He drew in a deep breath. Part of him missed the sensation and wanted more. It fired his blood and sent waves of need racing along his skin. He'd never felt anything remotely like it.

"You want it."

Enjoy this excerpt from
Healing Passion
Passions
© *Copyright Katherine Kingston, 2004*

The room was small but comfortable. The morning sunlight shone in through a window on his right, adding extra warmth to a space already heated by a low fire on the left. A table, a set of shelves, a cabinet with drawers and two chairs furnished the space. Each of the chairs bore a stuffed cushion, though those were the only feminine touches in an otherwise plain and businesslike space.

"Have a seat, if you will, Sir Thomas," Juliana said.

"If *you* will, my lady."

She smiled. "I should prefer to stand right now. I like to move around when I need to think."

Or when you're nervous. He didn't say it aloud, but the lady was clearly worried, and he didn't think that was due solely to being closed in a room with a man she barely knew and was too aware of. Did she fear the news he might be bringing about her husband?

He nodded acknowledgement and remained on his feet as well. "You've no doubt guessed I've come to ask about your husband. The king is concerned about him, as we've had no word of his whereabouts for nigh on a year."

"He is fighting with the Prince on the Continent, Sir Thomas, though I've had no word from him either and cannot say anything more of his exact location."

Sir Thomas drew a deep breath. "My lady, please forgive me if this discomposes you unduly, but I fear no one knows where he is or what he is now doing."

She gave him a quick, panic-stricken look and turned to face the window. "Is he not with the Prince in France?"

"The Prince is back in London, my lady. And Lord Groswick was not with him. In fact, the Prince has not seen him at any time, either on the Continent or here. He has no knowledge of his location. The king was concerned that one of his barons should disappear thus and asked me to investigate the matter."

Without moving her gaze from the scene outside the window, she reached out for the back of the chair nearby. Her palm slipped off and nearly unbalanced her, but she didn't turn around. She reached again and found the top edge. Before she clenched her fingers on it, he saw that her hand trembled.

"He did not join the Prince in France?" Her voice sounded thin and strained.

"Nay, my lady."

"And there's been no word at all from him?"

"Save you've received some message from him, nay."

"I have not." The words came out on a sigh.

"Have you had any word at all from him since he left the keep last year?"

She shook her head. "Nay."

"Know you how many men rode with him when he left here?"

For a moment she didn't answer. "Some twenty, I believe. He was to meet others along the way."

"Have you asked if any other families heard from others who went?"

"I've inquired. No one has heard anything."

"Why did you not send word to the king? Surely a year is a very long time to go with no message?"

Her fingers tightened on the chair. "Sir Thomas, had you known my husband, you would not think it so strange. He was a man of few words at the best of times."

"But to go a year..."

"'Tis not inconceivable."

The silence that followed was not comfortable. He hoped she would expand on why she thought her husband would remain silent, would even remain apart for so long from a wife as lovely and sweet as herself. She didn't add anything, however.

"Lady Juliana… I know not how to ask this delicately. How well did you know your husband?"

That brought her whirling around to face him. Some of the color had drained from her face, but there was also a look of fear, almost panic, in her eyes. She controlled it with an effort and made herself smile. The expression curved her mouth but left the rest of her face unmoved. "How well do most wives know their husbands? Perhaps they know them well after many years of living and working together, but I had only three years with my lord before he left. I knew the surface well enough and little of what was beneath."

"Did he ever give you reason to believe—or even think—he might be doing something other than going to battle?"

Her eyes unfocused for a moment as she thought. "Nay, I cannot remember him giving any such indication." She threaded her fingers together in agitation. "What shall we do? Have you talked to his uncle, the Earl of Everham? Perhaps he spent time there?"

"I spoke to him in London," Thomas said. "He knows no more of his nephew than do we."

She was starting to lose the struggle to control her expression. "I don't… What enquiries will you make now?"

He rubbed the back of his neck, wondering how his shoulder muscles could have gotten so tight so early in the day. "With your permission, I would speak to some of your people here. Perhaps someone heard a stray word that might give us a clue. I'd like also to speak to your crofters. Already I have spoken with many who live along the way from here to the sea, seeking someone who might have remembered seeing his party, but I have turned up naught. Not a one admits to knowing anything about them, or even recalls seeing him or his company pass."

"Does that not seem passing strange to you, Sir Thomas?"

"It does, my lady. Can you think of any reason why he might want to hide or disappear?"

Juliana shut her eyes for a moment. When she opened them she shook her head. "Nay. No reason."

"Did he not have enemies?"

She thought for a moment. "A few. I don't believe that any of those would have the nerve to attack him, save possibly from an ambush." Her sharp glance speared through him. "Sir Thomas…" She struggled to get the words out. "Do you think my husband yet lives?"

He stared at her, studying her expression. She had already more than half accepted that her husband was gone. She must have begun to wonder if it were so after so long a time of silence, but perhaps she did not want to believe. With him echoing her own suspicions, she could no longer avoid the likelihood of her husband's death. He could not read how she felt about that, other than that it left her afraid. The fear was natural and not surprising, for if Lord Groswick were dead, it put her future in grave doubt. It was his turn to find difficulty in speaking.

"Lady, you seem to be one who believes in plain words and open thoughts. I hope it is a courtesy I grant when I speak plainly in return. I do not believe your husband walks this Earth anymore, though I cannot begin to guess the method or location of his passing."

"Oh." The series of hard breaths that followed that small exclamation weren't quite sobs, but perhaps a shortness brought on by strong emotion. "Might he have been captured by enemies on the Continent?"

Thomas shook his head. "We would surely have heard. A baron is too valuable a pawn. There would have been a demand for ransom or exchange of prisoners."

"But then what could have happened?"

"An ambush, as you mentioned, is a possibility. Perhaps he was beset by robbers or brigands."

She nodded and rubbed her brow with a hand that shook. "What am I to do now?"

Her distress called to him. Without thinking or willing it, he moved toward her. "Lady Juliana. The king will see no harm comes to you. Should it be shown your husband is dead, the king will appoint a new lord for the lands and keep, but I'll have a word with him and request he have a care for you as well."

She didn't answer. Her thoughts seemed focused inward, and her fingers knotted together. She'd been carrying much responsibility and clearly doing it well, but he suspected this was a blow that could make the burden much greater. She braced herself on a long, hard inhalation. "I've managed heretofore. I shall continue to do so."

Sunlight coming in the window gleamed on a few dark brown curls that escaped from beneath her cap. It seemed to play around her slender, graceful form—such a slight figure to carry all the burdens she now bore. He couldn't help but admire her. She was just such a lady as he would want for himself.

A most unworthy thought crossed his mind. If Groswick were truly dead, the lady was free to marry again. All he'd learned inclined him to believe it was so. But should he harbor a hope that it was?

About the author:

Katherine welcomes mail from readers. You can write to her c/o Ellora's Cave Publishing at 1056 Home Avenue, Akron OH 44310-3502.

Why an electronic book?

We live in the Information Age—an exciting time in the history of human civilization in which technology rules supreme and continues to progress in leaps and bounds every minute of every hour of every day. For a multitude of reasons, more and more avid literary fans are opting to purchase e-books instead of paperbacks. The question to those not yet initiated to the world of electronic reading is simply: *why?*

1. *Price.* An electronic title at Ellora's Cave Publishing and Cerridwen Press runs anywhere from 40-75% less than the cover price of the <u>exact same title</u> in paperback format. Why? Cold mathematics. It is less expensive to publish an e-book than it is to publish a paperback, so the savings are passed along to the consumer.

2. *Space.* Running out of room to house your paperback books? That is one worry you will never have with electronic novels. For a low one-time cost, you can purchase a handheld computer designed specifically for e-reading purposes. Many e-readers are larger than the average handheld, giving you plenty of screen room. Better yet, hundreds of titles can be stored within your new library—a single microchip. (Please note that Ellora's Cave and Cerridwen Press does not endorse any specific brands. You can check our website at www.ellorascave.com or

www.cerridwenpress.com for customer recommendations we make available to new consumers.)

3. *Mobility.* Because your new library now consists of only a microchip, your entire cache of books can be taken with you wherever you go.

4. *Personal preferences are accounted for.* Are the words you are currently reading too small? Too large? Too...**ANNOYING**? Paperback books cannot be modified according to personal preferences, but e-books can.

5. *Instant gratification.* Is it the middle of the night and all the bookstores are closed? Are you tired of waiting days—sometimes weeks—for online and offline bookstores to ship the novels you bought? Ellora's Cave Publishing sells instantaneous downloads 24 hours a day, 7 days a week, 365 days a year. Our e-book delivery system is 100% automated, meaning your order is filled as soon as you pay for it.

Those are a few of the top reasons why electronic novels are displacing paperbacks for many an avid reader. As always, Ellora's Cave and Cerridwen Press welcomes your questions and comments. We invite you to email us at service@ellorascave.com, service@cerridwenpress.com or write to us directly at: 1056 Home Ave. Akron OH 44310-3502.

erridwen, the Celtic Goddess of wisdom, was the muse who brought inspiration to storytellers and those in the creative arts. Cerridwen Press encompasses the best and most innovative stories in all genres of today's fiction. Visit our site and discover the newest titles by talented authors who still get inspired - much like the ancient storytellers did, once upon a time.

Cerridwen Press

www.cerridwenpress.com

Discover for yourself why readers can't get enough of the multiple award-winning publisher Ellora's Cave. Whether you prefer e-books or paperbacks, be sure to visit EC on the web at www.ellorascave.com for an erotic reading experience that will leave you breathless.

www.ellorascave.com